Olivia Kidney
Stops for No One

originally titled
Olivia Kidney and the Exit Academy

ELLEN POTTER
ART BY PETER H. REYNOLDS

PUFFIN BOOKS

ACKNOWLEDGMENTS

Thanks to Daniel Hochman, a masterful skateboarder,
who taught me everything I know about an ollie.
Thanks also to Jessica Dougherty, whose insightful advice
helped me whip this book into shape.
And not a day goes by that I don't thank my *phenomenally* lucky stars
for my editor, Michael Green, and my agent, Alice Tasman.
–E. P.

PUFFIN BOOKS
Published by the Penguin Group
Penguin Young Readers Group, 345 Hudson Street, New York, New York 10014, U.S.A.
Penguin Group (Canada), 90 Eglinton Avenue, Suite 700, Toronto, Ontario, Canada M4P 2Y3
(a division of Pearson Penguin Canada Inc.)
Penguin Books Ltd, 80 Strand, London WC2R 0RL, England
Penguin Ireland, 25 St Stephen's Green, Dublin 2, Ireland (a division of Penguin Books Ltd)
Penguin Group (Australia), 250 Camberwell Road, Camberwell, Victoria 3124, Australia
(a division of Pearson Australia Group Pty Ltd)
Penguin Books India Pvt Ltd, 11 Community Centre, Panchsheel Park, New Delhi - 110 017, India
Penguin Group (NZ), 67 Apollo Drive, Mairangi Bay, Auckland 1311, New Zealand
(a division of Pearson New Zealand Ltd)
Penguin Books (South Africa) (Pty) Ltd, 24 Sturdee Avenue, Rosebank, Johannesburg 2196, South Africa

Registered Offices: Penguin Books Ltd, 80 Strand, London WC2R 0RL, England

First published in the United States of America by Philomel Books,
a division of Penguin Young Readers Group, 2005
Published by Puffin Books, a division of Penguin Young Readers Group, 2007

10 9 8 7 6 5 4

originally titled *Olivia Kidney and the Exit Academy*

THE LIBRARY OF CONGRESS HAS CATALOGED THE PHILOMEL EDITION AS FOLLOWS:
Potter, Ellen, date.
Olivia Kidney and the Exit Academy / Ellen Potter ; with illustrations by Peter H. Reynolds.
p. cm. Sequel to: Olivia Kidney. Summary: Twelve-year-old Olivia Kidney and her father move into a Manhattan brownstone that has a lagoon in the living room, hosts visiting strangers in the middle of the night, and is mysteriously close to the spirit world.
ISBN 0-399-24162-0 (hc)
[1. Death–Fiction. 2. Ghosts–Fiction. 3. Eccentrics and eccentricities–Fiction. 4. New York (N.Y.)–Fiction.]
I. Reynolds, Peter, date. ill. II. Title. PZ7.P8518Om 2005 [Fic]–dc2004009090

Puffin Books ISBN 978-0-14-240772-1

Printed in the United States of America

Designed by Gina DiMassi. The text is set in Worcester Round.

For Daryl
–E. P.

To Bill Norris,
a man who believes, like Olivia,
in possibilities.
–P. R.

One

Olivia Kidney's suitcase was made of a tired-looking green- and white-striped canvas, with a zipper that didn't close all the way and a rip beginning to widen along its seam. She probably should have thrown it away, but it had moved her in and out of many apartments over the years, and she felt sort of attached to it.

At the moment it was bulging with nearly all of her belongings, and she was struggling to haul it up the L-shaped front steps of a grim-looking brownstone building.

"I don't like it," she said. In her other hand she was gripping an old wooden toolbox.

"You always say that in the beginning," her father, George Kidney, replied.

It was true. Olivia always hated the feeling of being in a new home, and of not knowing what sort of place it was. But her father was constantly being fired from his jobs as building superintendent, so they had to keep moving. It wasn't that George Kidney didn't *try* to do a good job. It was just that he wasn't very good at the job that he did. At the last apartment building, when he attempted to fix the broken faucet in someone's bathtub, the water came gushing out in torrents. The whole apartment and the five apartments below that one were flooded. George was fired the very next day.

Olivia gazed up at the brownstone warily. "It looks like it wants us to go away and leave it alone," she said.

The building was four stories high, with tall windows. Some of the windows that faced the street had small balconies perched outside. The stones of the building were large and formidable, and the color of mud. Not nice mud. The kind of mud that has been festering in some dark, moist, hidden place for years and years.

Up and down 84th Street were rows of brownstones, many of them with the same L-shaped front steps and heavy bricks. But the stones were pleasant-colored browns—like the chestnut and deep bay browns of horses. And nearly all of them had bright early summer flowers growing from flower boxes in front of the windows, and generally looked very welcoming. Not a single one of them was as gloomy as number 917 West 84th Street.

They reached the top step and George Kidney put down his suitcase, which was in even worse shape than Olivia's. A U-Haul moving van parked in front of the building held the rest of their belongings.

George pressed the buzzer. Olivia gripped her bag and the toolbox tighter in her fists.

"He could at least put some flowers out front." Olivia looked at the empty stone flower boxes, with drips of yellowish dried bird droppings running down the sides.

"Maybe he'll let you plant some," George said brightly.

"No, thanks. It's *his* house."

They waited another few minutes and then George pressed the buzzer again. Still no one answered. George turned the doorknob, just to try, and found that the door was open.

"He leaves his front door open? In New York City?" Olivia cried.

"It just shows that he's trusting."

"It just shows that no one in their right mind would *want* to go into his house."

"Olivia . . ." George looked at his daughter warningly. "Attitude."

"I have one."

"Well, try to get a better one."

As soon as they stepped inside the entrance hallway, their feet sank a full inch into the depths of carpeting. The carpet ran the length of the hallway and was woven with an extraordinarily intricate design.

"I guess we should take our shoes off," George whispered. Then he put his bag back down and began to untie his shoes.

"I'm keeping mine on."

"You'll track dirt," George hissed.

"Then he shouldn't put such a fancy rug where everyone walks," Olivia hissed back.

"Is someone there?" a voice called from a distance. It seemed to be coming from the room to their left, which was shut off by a pair of white double doors with an ornate plaster carving above it in the shape of three horses galloping in a line. "If not, kindly leave."

George removed his shoes. Against the luxurious rug, they looked even more scuffed than usual, Olivia thought. Then George tried, unsuccessfully, to smooth down his wild sandy-colored hair. He glanced uncertainly at Olivia.

"You look fine, Dad," she said. Oddly, she too felt suddenly self-conscious, as though they were going to be presented to someone very important. Olivia put down her suitcase to push her hair out of her eyes, but still kept a tight grip on the handle of the toolbox. She looked down to check that her fly was closed. It was.

George turned the gold door handle and they both walked in. For a full minute they stood there in silence, dumbstruck.

Taking up most of the room was a huge, sparkling lagoon, which narrowed at the far end, twisted around a corner, and disappeared. The lagoon was fully furnished with a sofa and armchairs and little end tables, and a few lamps and bookcases; but each piece of furniture was floating on its own little raft, and they bobbed gently and rearranged themselves as they slowly drifted. A narrow, raised marble walkway surrounded the water, across which several cats slunk, eyeing Olivia and George suspiciously. Great marble columns sprouted out of the walkway and touched the ceiling, which was gilded with gold.

"Holy cow," Olivia whispered.

Suddenly, a long, shallow black boat glided around the sharp bend at the opposite end of the room and entered the lagoon. There were two people in the boat. One of them was a young blond man dressed in a cream-colored linen suit, reclining on a heap of pillows on the bottom of the boat. His feet, which were bare, were crossed and resting on the boat's edge. The other occupant, the one who was strenuously working the oars, was a tall, slender young woman in a maid's uniform, with cropped black hair that looked slept on—in a fashionable way.

"Hello," George ventured.

"And hello back!" the blond man called out. He smiled at George as if he had known him all his life and had only just been wondering when good old George would come and visit him again. The man was very handsome, with the sort of face that you keep looking at to make sure that it is really as handsome as you think it is. Olivia thought of Renee, a girl who lived in the last building her father had worked in. Boy, Renee would be swallowing her gum right about now, Olivia thought.

"My name is Ansel Plover," the blond man said. "And this is the lovely Nora." The woman had stopped rowing, and the boat was bobbing slightly in the middle of the lagoon. "Well, this is an odd time of day for a visit. Most people prefer the middle of the night, but there are always exceptions in this business." Ansel looked over at Olivia and frowned. "Oh dear . . . a child . . ."

"See, Dad. He doesn't like children. Let's go," Olivia said, and she grabbed George by the elbow.

"But I *adore* children," Ansel protested. "Especially ones with bad tempers. Nora, have them climb aboard."

Nora steered the boat to the edge. The black boat was lacquered to a high sheen. It reminded Olivia of a coffin.

Ansel stood up and extended his hand. George took it first and, still in his socks, stepped gingerly into the narrow boat, lurching forward when he felt it wobble.

"Steady . . . have a sit, there you go," Ansel said as George sat down on one of the pillows.

"Now you," Ansel said, putting his hand out toward Olivia. She hesitated.

"Come on," George encouraged, already looking happily settled in. "It's actually pretty comfortable."

"I'm fine where I am," Olivia replied, gripping her toolbox so tightly that her fingers ached.

"You can take your treasure with you, love, there's plenty of room," Ansel said. The fact that he recognized that her toolbox was a treasure softened her somewhat, and, reluctantly, she accepted his help aboard and settled beside her father on the pillows.

"A house filled with water–it's ingenious!" George said amicably.

"It's nice, isn't it?" Ansel agreed. "It's based on an ancient Egyptian tradition–"

"Don't let him fleece you," Nora interrupted. "It's based on the fact that there was a leak in the roof." Then Nora pushed off with her oars, maneuvering the boat around in a circle, so they were headed back toward the way they had come.

"Well, technically, of course, Nora is correct. It did start out as a leak. It was rather a mess at first, but it seemed like such a bother to pump the water *out,* and so much easier to put more water *in*. Now, what can I do for you?"

"Do for *us?*" George shook his head in confusion. "We came . . . you asked us to come . . . a live-in situation . . . that is . . . Oh, maybe there's been some mistake . . ."

"Oh, no, no, no! No mistake at all!" Ansel patted him on the back. "A live-in situation. We haven't done that before. An excellent idea."

The boat sailed through the narrow opening and into a sort of canal, which snaked around and passed beneath a low, arched ceiling, so low that you could hardly stand without bumping your head. Here and there the canal opened out to other rooms, where the furniture also floated.

"Let's see," Ansel pondered. "We can put you in the rooms on the fourth floor, so the other people won't bother you." Then he suddenly sat up and cried, "Look out, Nora, she's on the loose again!"

Up ahead, floating out of one of the rooms was a toilet, bobbing idly on the soft waves. Nora quickly steered the boat to the left and squeezed by the toilet without hitting it.

"You've got to put an anchor on that thing, or it's going to kill somebody one day," Nora complained.

"What other people?" Olivia asked Ansel.

"Excuse me?" he said.

"You said you'd put us on the fourth floor so the other people won't bother us." The house had seemed perfectly empty, except for Ansel, Nora, and the cats.

"Oh, they're no one to be concerned about." Ansel waved his hand dismissively. "Just our evening visitors. Anyway, your rooms are way up on the tippy-top of the house, and they hardly ever venture up there. Here we are."

They had stopped at a circular stairway made of wrought iron that rose out of the water and stretched up through the ceiling. There were other boats moored around the stairs, tied to wooden poles that poked out of the water, one of which Nora now threw a rope around.

"By the way," Ansel said, "what are your names?"

"We're the Kidneys," George said, sending a confused glance toward Olivia. "George and Olivia."

"*The Kidneys?!* Of course! Well, well, well, then!" Ansel cried, as though George had told him the most extraordinary thing. "Nora will show you to your rooms. Mind your step. There are snapping turtles lurking. My mother stocked the pond with them last year. She said it would remind me to take my life more seriously. I don't know as it's worked, however."

They carefully stepped from the boat to the stairs, and Nora led the way up. The stairs were so steep that they made Olivia's thighs ache, but she was relieved that there was no elevator. Olivia hated elevators. Mostly because she was scared of them. They all had some kind of terrifying quirk—a shudder or a violent up-and-down bobble when they stopped, or a threatening grinding sound that made you wonder if the cable was going to snap at any second. The thought of a cable snapping terrified Olivia so much that her father, to calm her fears, had even called an elevator company to find out how many times a cable had snapped and killed someone in New York City (since 1857 there had been only nine instances). But that still didn't convince Olivia that elevators were safe.

On the fourth-floor landing, Nora opened the door and they walked into what was clearly the attic, since the ceiling sloped at odd angles. There was a door on the right side of the hallway and another on the left.

"Take your pick." Nora shrugged, and left. For a moment Olivia and George did not move. They looked at each other. Olivia raised her eyebrows and George raised his in response.

"Well, this is different," George said. He was trying to make his voice sound optimistic, but Olivia could tell he was worried. "We've never lived in a real house before."

"And you can't flood it, since it's already flooded," Olivia added.

"That's not helpful, Olivia."

She opened the door on the right and immediately let out a hiss of surprise. Taking up the bulk of the room was a huge canopied bed. It looked like something that a princess would sleep in. Olivia put down her toolbox, walked up to the bed, and touched the embroidered turquoise bedspread, then ran her fingers through the gauzy white drapes hanging from the canopy. She flopped down onto the bed, belly first, then flipped over and spread her arms wide.

"You could fit ten of me on this thing," she said.

"This room's yours then," George said, and he went to have a look at the other room.

Olivia lay still for a moment and looked around. Beside the bed was a little nightstand, on top of which was a squat vase of puffy pink and white flowers. Propped up against the vase was a large square envelope. Olivia sat up. She leaned over and picked up the envelope. It had no name on it, but it wasn't sealed either, so naturally she opened it. Inside was a card with the night sky on its front, and stars raised up in shiny bits of foil. Olivia opened the card and read the printed message: *Happy Birthday, Uncle!* Beneath that, in a neat, square handwriting was written:

> Dear Olivia,
>
> Sorry about the "Happy Birthday" thing. I just happened to like the picture on the front. I have one thing to tell you:
>
> Don't jump to conclusions.
>
> Also, don't jump up and down in the bedroom. The floorboards are not the strongest, and you do have a tendency to stomp around like a 300-pound man in clogs.

"That is *so* rude!" Olivia frowned. "And how does he know how I walk, anyway!?"

"What do you think, Sweetpea?" George walked in, smiling widely. "Pretty fancy stuff for us Kidneys, huh?"

"I guess. Hey, Dad. Do I walk heavily?"

"You know what Christopher used to say?" George said.

Olivia shook her head. Christopher was her older brother, who had died last summer.

"He said that you walked as though you had something very important to do in this world . . ."

Olivia smiled a little.

". . . and as if you had soda cans strapped to your feet."

Two

After they had moved their suitcases and the dozen or so boxes into the house, Olivia decided to explore the neighborhood. That was her favorite part of moving to a new place. Even though the building she'd lived in before was only ten blocks uptown, this neighborhood felt completely different. It was quieter and prettier, and there were more trees on the street.

As Olivia walked down the brownstone's front steps, she nearly tripped on a small figure. It was a thin little girl, about seven or eight years old, with very short, brown hair and wearing a plaid skirt and a blue blouse–the kind of outfit private-school girls wear. She was crouching on one of the upper steps, evidently trying to hide from someone.

The girl looked up at Olivia and whispered, "Who are you?"

"Who are *you?*" Olivia retorted.

"Venice," the girl whispered, after a hesitation.

"That's a place, not a name."

"I know. I hate it. They made me change my real name."

"Who did?" Olivia asked.

"The school." The girl pointed at the brownstone next door. Beside the door, above the buzzer, was a bronze sign that said MS. BENDER'S SCHOOL FOR SUPERIOR CHILDREN.

Olivia narrowed her eyes at the girl. "Superior"? The little girl didn't look superior. But the one thing Olivia had learned during the past year was that people were rarely what they seemed to be at first sight.

"Who are you hiding from?" Olivia asked.

The girl looked up at her with wide eyes. "The hairdresser. She came to dye my hair blond."

The door of the brownstone next door opened and a woman wearing a white smock and a pair of yellow-stained plastic gloves peered out.

"Have you seen a small girl around here?" the woman asked Olivia. "Yay high? Dark hair?"

"Nope," Olivia said definitively. The woman grunted and went back inside. The girl by Olivia's feet waited a moment, then stood up.

"Thanks," the little girl said, and she ran her hand through her hair. "So . . . do you know *him?*"

"Who's *him?*"

"Ansel Plover." The girl's eyes widened dramatically as she jerked her thumb toward Olivia's new home.

"Not very well. Why?"

"It's just that I've never seen anyone come out of his house during the day," the girl said. "I've only seen people go in or come out at night."

"What sort of people?" Olivia asked.

The girl shrugged. "All different sorts. I can see the front of his house from the window by my bed, and people are coming and going all night long."

From inside the brownstone next door a woman's strident voice began to shout, "Venice! Venice Smithers! You are to come and have your hair dyed this instant!"

"Run!" Venice cried. She grabbed Olivia's arm and yanked her down the stairs. For a tiny thing, she was surprisingly strong and fast, and Olivia found herself being dragged along, up the street, heading toward Central Park. It was only when they entered the park that Venice let go of Olivia's arm and slowed down somewhat, though her spidery legs maintained a ground-covering stride.

"So, Venice—" Olivia started.

"Call me Frannie. That's my real name."

"Okay, Frannie then." Olivia was relieved. Venice was such a stupid name. "So what do you know about Ansel?"

"Well, the other day our riding instructor told Ms. Bender that she thought Ansel was handsome and devastatingly charming. And Ms. Bender said, 'Oh yes, he's charming all right. But underneath, the man is a poisonous spider–mad, bad, and dangerous.' Ms. Bender is afraid of him. She thinks he's seriously crazy. And if you've ever met Ms. Bender, you'd know she doesn't scare easily."

Olivia looked at her skeptically. "How do you know all of this?"

"Let's just say I pay attention," Frannie said somewhat evasively. "Most people don't, you know." It sounded very precocious coming out of the mouth of someone so young. Perhaps she *was* superior, Olivia thought.

"Plus," Frannie added as though she were reading Olivia's mind, "people think of me as a little girl. That means they aren't so careful about what they say around me."

"I hate to break this to you, but you *are* a little girl," Olivia said.

Frannie snorted. "I'm probably older than you are," she said.

"Don't be ridiculous," Olivia said. They were passing the Delacorte Theater now, in front of which was a bronze statue of two young lovers who were smoothly entwined, almost kissing.

"Romeo and Juliet," Frannie commented as they passed it. "Now *they* were ridiculous! Oh, don't get me wrong—I used to love reading that play. I checked it out of the school library so many times that the librarian banned me from taking it out for six months. So I hid it behind the arts and crafts books and read it during lunch period. But I kind of outgrew it. I mean, the two of them were just moping around, making a big drama out of everything. If they hadn't died in the end, they would have gotten sick of each other."

Olivia frowned at Frannie. "How old are you anyway?"

"Around the same as them," Frannie nodded toward Romeo and Juliet. "Fourteen." She smiled at Olivia's shocked face. "I haven't grown since I was seven," Frannie explained. "Not even an inch. The doctors don't know why. Personally, I think it's very Darwinian."

"Is that a disease?"

"Darwinian," Frannie repeated as though Olivia were an idiot. "As in Charles Darwin. As in Survival of the Fittest."

Frannie made a small sigh of exasperation when Olivia still looked perplexed. "Okay," she explained, "you know how there are insects that are camouflaged to look exactly like twigs so their enemies won't notice them? Well, in my case, I camouflaged myself by being especially small."

"Why don't you want to be noticed?"

"Let's just say that my mother has lousy taste in boyfriends, and sometimes it's safer not to be noticed. The doctors don't believe my theory, of course."

"Is that why you're in a school for special kids? Because you don't grow?" Olivia asked after a moment. She suddenly felt awkward around Frannie. She couldn't treat her like a little kid, yet it was hard to treat her like a person who was two years older than herself.

"Ms. Bender's? The kids in that school aren't special," Frannie replied.

"But the sign said 'for Superior Children.' "

"Nah, all the kids there are totally average. A lot of them are less than average, if you want to know the truth. It's just that their parents want everyone to *think* their kids are superior. Like my mother, for instance. She's engaged to this guy, Claude Vondychomps. He's got piles of dough. Dumb as a box of rocks, too, from the way Mom describes him, but not a bad person. Mom told him she was a Hungarian countess. She's really a dog groomer from the Bronx. I don't think she even knows where Hungary is. Frankly, I doubt Claude knows where Hungary is either. But he's not the one who needs to believe her. It's Claude's father, Mr. Vondychomps, whom she's trying to impress. He's this ultra-snobby old guy, and if he thinks we're phonies, he won't let his son marry my mom, so she put me and my sister in Ms. Bender's school to whip us into shape. Ms. Bender specializes in cases like this."

"What do they teach you?"

"Oh, everything. How to eat and walk and say things like, 'It's time for a brisk caaaaanter on my pony, what.' "

"I didn't say anything."

"What?"

"You said, *what,*" Olivia told her.

"They teach us to say *what* after you make a statement. It's supposed to make you sound clever."

"I think it makes you sound like you have a hearing problem," Olivia said.

"I know it. Anyway, I'm doing pretty well in all my classes, but my older sister Dijon is having a hard time. She can't get rid of her Bronx accent and she's allergic to horses and Ms. Bender is awful to her. My mom's going to introduce me to her fiancé and his father first, to soften them up before they meet Dijon. Hey, what time is it?" Frannie asked.

Olivia checked her watch. "Two fifteen."

"Okay. I guess it's safe to go back. The hairdresser has probably given up by now."

"Why are they trying to dye your hair anyway?" Olivia asked.

"Oh, they always do it right before your first meeting with the fiancé. They dye all the kids' hair the same color—'butter-blond.' It's supposed to look aristocratic. But I won't let them do it. I simply refuse. It's completely undignified."

Olivia looked down at Frannie. She really did seem to be a dignified little person, and Olivia could not picture her with butter-blond hair.

"Well, so long, Olivia," Frannie said. "And if I were you, I'd lock my door at night. We hear strange noises coming out of Ansel Plover's house in the evenings. He has some weird parties, I think."

Frannie rushed off, her skinny, buglike legs racing although she wasn't actually running. Olivia was a little sorry to see her go—she was sort of an interesting kid.

Olivia ambled over to the bank of the pond by the

Delacorte Theater, checking the grass carefully before she sat down. This news about Ansel worried her. Was he actually dangerous? She would definitely lock her door tonight, but she doubted it would help her sleep any easier. She shook her head crossly—why couldn't her father hold on to a job for longer than a few months? Why did he have to be such a bad handyman?

"Perhaps you should consider a career change, Mr. Kidney." This had been said a month before by the Princepessa Christina Lilli, an old, exiled princess who had been one of Olivia's neighbors at their previous apartment building. Although the Princepessa was cranky at times, she had plenty of common sense.

"But what else would I do?" George had asked.

"Hmm. Well . . . think back to when you were a little boy, Mr. Kidney. What did you want to do when you grew up?"

George had thought for a moment. "I wanted to be a cowboy."

"Pity." The Princepessa had shaken her head.

The day after George Kidney was fired from the last apartment building, Olivia spotted an envelope that had been shoved beneath their apartment door. She opened it up and read:

Dear Mr. Kidney,

You have come highly recommended as a handyman with extraordinary talent, a pleasant personality, and good dental hygiene. I want to hire you immediately as a live-in superintendent in my brownstone at 917 West 84th Street. Enclosed please find $1,000.00 in advance payment for your first two weeks of work. You can move in on the first of July. I eagerly await your arrival.

There was no signature on the letter, and in the envelope were ten crisp $100 bills.

"One door closes and another one opens!" George said excitedly when Olivia showed him the note. "I'm calling U-Haul right now." He picked up the phone and started to dial, but Olivia grabbed the phone out of his hands.

"Hold on a second," Olivia said. "Let's think about this. Who do you think slipped the note under our door?"

George shrugged. "Maybe the Princepessa had something to do with it. What does it matter? It's an opportunity." He took the phone out of Olivia's hands and began to dial.

But when Olivia asked the Princepessa if it was she who had slipped the note under the door, the Princepessa had snapped, "I do *not* slip notes under doors. It stirs up all the dust on the floor. And besides, it's the act of a coward!"

"I was just asking," Olivia shot back.

"And what if I 'just asked' you if you were a Philistine?"

"I wouldn't know what you were talking about," Olivia replied.

"Then we understand each other," the Princepessa said. "Now come inside and we'll play a round of pinochle."

"I don't know how."

"Even better. We'll play for money."

THREE

Olivia unpacked her suitcase and grudgingly put her clothes into the dresser. On the bottom of the suitcase were half a dozen books, all taken from her brother Christopher's bookcase. They weren't the normal sort of books that most twelve-year-old girls read. These were books about ghosts and magic and the afterlife. Her favorite book was called *Chatting With Ghosts,* written by Madame Brenda, a famous psychic, and it was a sort of how-to book about contacting dead people. It was her favorite book partly because she had actually met the author a few months before. Madame Brenda was not at all what Olivia imagined a psychic would be like. She had tomato-red hair and she was obsessed with the shoe sales at Bloomingdale's and she lived down in Florida. But she really *could* contact ghosts–Olivia had seen it with her own eyes. Plus, Madame Brenda had been the one who'd told Olivia that she too had the gift to contact the dead.

That made Olivia think of Branwell. She had met him

last winter, and he had been the first friend she'd made in a long, long time. She felt a stab of sadness, and wondered for the umpteenth time how he was, and if she'd ever hear from him again.

After all her clothes and books were put away, Olivia opened up the old toolbox. Inside were two dolls–a brother and a sister doll that looked exactly like Olivia and her brother, Christopher. Olivia cherished these dolls as her prize possessions. She looked around the room for a safe spot for the toolbox, and settled on a shelf in the back of her closet.

That night Olivia lay in the tremendous canopy bed, which made her feel especially small. She had locked her door, as Frannie advised, and stayed awake for a long time, listening in the darkness for odd sounds or footsteps clanking on the iron stairs. But except for the occasional passing car outside and the soft snoring of her father across the hall, it was perfectly silent.

Sleep tugged at her, gently but persistently, and finally she gave in, only to awake again suddenly, feeling as though she had been startled out of sleep but not knowing why. She lay still and listened, blinking up at the ceiling. Then she heard it: "How dare you! How dare you make me come here in the middle of the night!"

The voice sounded like it was coming from outside.

Olivia got out of bed—actually she had to roll three times across the mattress before she reached the edge and stepped down—opened the window, and leaned out. In front of the brownstone, standing beneath a streetlight, was a fat man with a tuft of curly rusty-red hair. His face was clearly illuminated by the light above, and Olivia could see he had a long, thin nose and a thick lower lip, and that he was staring up at Ansel's brownstone with wild, furious eyes. He seemed to look in her direction suddenly, and Olivia pulled back a little so he wouldn't see her.

Olivia heard the front door open and Ansel's pleasant voice saying, "Hello, my dear man. Did you have any trouble finding us?"

"How dare you!!" the man roared. "I will not accept this, I promise you! I'll call my lawyer!"

"Oh my, you are a fiery one, aren't you?" Ansel said good-naturedly. "Step up and come inside. You'll see that it's not at all what you're expecting. Most people find the experience thoroughly delightful!"

"I won't do this, I won't! You can't force me! I'll have you arrested!"

"Frederick . . . it *is* Frederick, isn't it? Come inside. You can call the police and have me arrested afterward. What do you say, friend?"

There was silence, and Frederick's head dipped down as though he were considering. Then Olivia saw his heavy round shoulders shaking, heaving up and down, and she realized that he was crying. Ansel walked down the stairs and put an arm around the man's shoulder.

"That's my boy, Frederick. Nothing to be afraid of. In we go." Ansel gently ushered Frederick up the stairs, and then Olivia heard the door click shut.

She pulled her head back inside her bedroom and shut the window. She listened hard for voices, but the house was completely silent now. What had just happened? What had Ansel done to infuriate the man?

I don't like this, she thought nervously as she climbed back into bed. I wish I were back in the last apartment house. I wish Dad wasn't such a lousy super. Her hopes lifted at this last thought, however. Certainly, it wouldn't be long before her father would bungle something up and get himself fired from here too. If there was one thing in her life she could always count on, it was that.

Olivia pulled the covers over her nose. Gradually her muscles began to relax and she once again began to fall asleep, until a bloodcurdling cawing sound, like the shriek of a bird of prey, erupted from somewhere downstairs. She sat bolt upright in her bed and put her knuckle to her lips to suppress a cry. Then the house was silent again.

Dad better start bungling ASAP, she thought.

In the morning she packed up her duffel bag and made her way down the winding, narrow staircase, pausing at the third-floor landing. Putting down her duffel bag, she placed her ear against the door, listening. Somewhere within, there was a faint sound of rustling. She pressed her ear harder to the door. The rustling seemed to grow louder, and then the door opened suddenly, throwing Olivia off balance. As she stumbled to her knees, her hand shot out in front of her, grabbing hold of a handful of frilly white material to keep herself from falling. Raising her eyes, she found herself looking up at Nora, whose apron she was now gripping.

"Hands off the goods, kid." Nora sidestepped to get out of Olivia's grasp. "What's wrong with you?" Nora asked as Olivia got to her feet. "You been drinking?"

"I'm only twelve!" Olivia cried.

"Then you shouldn't be drinking," Nora said firmly, and she started down the stairs. "Don't worry, I won't tell your dad. I was pretty wild when I was younger too. Of course, I wasn't drinking when I was *twelve*–"

"Neither was–"

"But I used to get into my share of trouble, believe me," Nora said.

"I only fell because–"

" 'Born bad,' that's what my parents always said about me, and I guess they were right. But I calmed down after I started working for Ansel."

When they reached the bottom of the stairs, Nora nimbly leapt into one of the moored boats.

"Get in, kid, I'll give you a lift," Nora said as she untied the mooring ropes. Even though Olivia stepped into the boat very carefully, it still tipped sharply to one side, and she let out an involuntary squeal.

"I'll never get used to this," Olivia muttered.

Out in the lagoon Ansel and George were sitting in a boat, each one holding a fishing rod. George grinned sheepishly at his daughter. He was clearly enjoying himself.

"Shouldn't you be working, Dad?" Olivia asked nervously.

"I've commanded your father to fish this morning," Ansel said imperiously. "There is a giant trout in this lagoon, and I am determined to catch him."

Nora rowed to the edge of the lagoon, and Olivia picked up her duffel bag and cautiously stepped off the boat and onto the marble walkway. She glanced back at her father and frowned. If George was going to bungle something, he'd have to start doing some work.

"You really should have my father work on the plumbing," Olivia said to Ansel. "That's his specialty. He's a genius at plumbing."

George blushed. "Well, I don't know about genius . . ."

"Don't be modest, George," Ansel said. Then his eyes rested on Olivia's duffel bag. "You aren't leaving us, dear Olivia, are you?" He sounded genuinely pained. "But you simply mustn't leave! We can't manage without you!"

It wasn't true, of course, and Olivia knew it. Ansel was just being charming. But, she had to admit, he sounded *so* earnest. *Mad, bad, and dangerous.* She must remember that!

"Where are you going, Sweetpea?" George asked.

"I've got plans for the day," Olivia said lightly. One of the cats sidled up to her and rubbed against her ankle.

"Visiting a friend?" George asked. In fact, Olivia didn't really have any friends. She had been shuffled from school to school so often that she was never in one place long enough to make friends.

"Yeah, I'm visiting a friend," Olivia replied. In a way, it was not a lie.

• • •

Outside, the day was warm. She imagined that the air smelled a little fresher in this neighborhood, simply because Central Park was so close. She sat on the front steps and looked up and down the street. It was perfectly empty at the moment. Olivia closed her eyes.

When she had first started contacting Christopher on a regular basis, she had concentrated so hard that her jaw would clench tight and her face would grow hot. And although she usually managed to reach him, the connection was staticky and they usually got cut off too soon. Afterward she always suffered from a headache.

But as she practiced, she realized that she didn't have to work that hard to connect with him. Really, it was a simple matter of relaxing and imagining her brother as clearly as possible–his face, his voice, the way he smelled. Then she'd feel a warmth in her stomach, and often she could see something out of the corner of her eye. It was almost as though a piece of dust were floating by her ear, but every time she swiveled around to look at it, it was gone.

"Hey, kiddo," Christopher said now. She heard his voice in her head the same way that she heard her own thoughts. Only they were Christopher's thoughts.

"Hey, Christopher." When she replied, she didn't talk out loud; she merely "thought" her replies, and he heard them. It was a tricky thing to do in public. When she first started talking to him in front of other people, she sometimes laughed or nodded her head during their silent conversation, and people would stare at her as if she were crazy. But Olivia had since learned how to keep her face neutral. "I was thinking we could spend the day together," she said. "Are you busy?"

"Not until four-thirty."

"What's happening at four-thirty?" Olivia asked.

"Barry," Christopher said glumly.

"What's a Barry?" Olivia asked.

"Barry is a 'who,' not a 'what.' Barry McFarkle. He just arrived last week, and he's already driving me crazy. Why do I always get assigned to the hard cases?"

"Probably because you're so patient."

"Yeah? Well, Barry might put an end to that. He's a thrill seeker. Which is fine. I mean, hey, I liked a little danger in my cereal, too, when I was alive. But Barry is something else. You know how he died? He sat in a lawn chair and had a friend tie two hundred helium balloons to it, just to see if it would float. And since Barry weighs about as much as a wet cat, the thing actually took off. Barry floated clear across the state of Maine and was cruising a hundred feet over the Atlantic Ocean when the balloons started popping from the pressure. And plop! There goes Barry, straight into the Atlantic. He said that, as he was falling, he realized he should have thought the experiment through a little better."

"He doesn't sound too bright."

"You think? Anyway, death hasn't seemed to cure him of the thrill-seeking habit. If anything, it's made him worse. He says that since he's already dead, he's got nothing to lose, so . . . woohoo! Let's party! I've spent the past week tossing him off cliffs in a wooden barrel."

"If I were you, I'd just refuse."

"Can't. It's part of his therapy. After a while he's supposed to realize that his behavior is ridiculous, and then he can move on to more important things."

"What if he never does?" Olivia asked.

"Then I'll toss *myself* off a cliff in a wooden barrel! Hey, what's in the duffel bag, kiddo?"

Olivia smiled. "A surprise." She stood up, lifted the bag, and said, "Ready?"

"Lead the way."

She headed toward the park, but kept her eyes peeled for things that might amuse Christopher. It could be anything: a little dog in a baby stroller, a man with a silver picture frame around his head, two cabdrivers fighting in the middle of the street. Christopher said that one of the things he really missed about earth was New York City and all the chaos and craziness. So once a week, Olivia would take her brother on a "field trip." That's what he called it, at least.

"But couldn't you visit New York City on your own too?" Olivia once asked him.

"Sure. A lot of spirits float around the earth to check things out or just to take a little vacation. 'Tourists,' we call them. A tourist can see things okay, but they can't really *feel* them. When I'm with you, I can *feel* things. If *you* eat a hot dog, *I* can taste it. If you think something is funny, I *feel* the funny."

On Columbus Avenue, Olivia carefully perused the stores and the people, looking for something interesting. She paused briefly at a pet store, in front of which was a large wooden crate with a sign painted on it: CAUTION! BABY RATTLERS! Olivia walked up to the crate and peered in through the wire grate on top of it. Inside were pink and blue plastic rattles for babies. Olivia rolled her eyes.

"Ha, ha," she said dryly, feeling duped. But Christopher was laughing anyway, which pleased her.

Just off Central Park West she entered the park. To the left was a playground where little kids were zipping around like the metal balls in a pinball machine. Olivia felt a small tug in the direction of the playground, so she knew that Christopher was looking at it.

"Dad and I used to take you to this playground when you were little," Christopher said.

"Not Mom?" Olivia asked.

"She didn't like playgrounds. She said all the activity made her dizzy." Their mother had divorced George a few years before and moved to California. Every so often, she'd call Olivia and tell her how warm it was there and that she'd send her a plane ticket very soon, but no plane ticket ever showed up. And, to be completely honest, Olivia wasn't all that sorry.

"I remember one time you climbed that thing." He nudged her attention to the playground's large metal climbing ladder shaped like an upside-down U. "You were only three–too little to be up there–but before we could stop you, you were at the top of it. Then, once you were up there, you became scared out of your wits, and you were staring at me with these great big terrified eyes. I wanted to climb up and get you down, but Dad wouldn't let me. He said, 'Just smile and wave at her. If she thinks you're scared for her, she'll fall. Don't worry. She'll find her own way down.' So I gritted my teeth and smiled and waved, even though I kept picturing you tumbling through the air.

But Dad was right. When you saw that I wasn't afraid for you, you got your courage back and made it all the way across. Hey, do you smell that?!"

Olivia inhaled a warm, yeasty scent.

"Pretzels," she said. She searched the grassy slope and found a pretzel vendor with his little metal cart a few yards off. "Want one?" she asked.

"With mustard."

She wasn't a big fan of mustard, but she bought a hot pretzel tucked in a napkin and squirted mustard until there was nothing left in the bottle and it made a little farty noise.

"Geez, that's disgusting, Olivia!" Christopher said.

"It wasn't me, it was the mustard!" She said this out loud by accident, and the man selling pretzels smirked.

Olivia turned bright red and quickly walked away.

"Take a bite," Christopher urged.

"Say you're sorry."

"I'm sorry."

Olivia took a big bite. As she chewed, she felt Christopher focusing on the taste, until he finally cried out, "Now, that's a slice of heaven!"

"Can't you get pretzels after you're dead?" Olivia asked.

"Sure. But they don't taste the same without a body. Take another bite, will you?"

Olivia didn't like the mustard, but tried not to pay too much attention to it. They walked in silence as Olivia chewed and Christopher tasted.

"So how's the new place?" Christopher asked after the pretzel was finished. "You haven't said a word about it."

Olivia had been deliberately blocking Ansel from her mind. Partly because she didn't know what to make of things, and partly because whenever she was worried or anxious, Christopher could feel it. He said it felt similar to air turbulence on a plane, which couldn't be very much fun.

"It's fine," Olivia said. She quickly tried to think about things that really *were* fine in order to avoid the turbulence: her sneakers were fine (no splits along the seams), the latest checkup at the dentist was fine (no cavities, just a tiny one threatening) . . .

"You're a bad liar, Olivia Kidney," Christopher said.

Olivia was about to protest but gave in and admitted, "Okay. I don't like it."

"You never like new things," Christopher said.

"But this place is really weird, Christopher! Last night, a man came to the door screaming that he was going to call the police and have the owner arrested."

"Did he?"

"Well, no . . . I guess not, since Ansel was still there in

the morning. But Ansel is supposed to be crazy, Christopher. I mean seriously crazy!"

Christopher was silent for a moment. "Some people said that about you, too, a few months back."

It was true, which annoyed her, and she didn't reply.

"All I'm saying is, use your gray matter, kiddo."

"Do you know something about Ansel that I don't know?" Olivia asked suspiciously.

"Nope, not a thing. I'm not that advanced yet."

"Well, can't you just . . . I don't know . . . check with your supervisor?"

"It doesn't work that way," Christopher said patiently.

"You can't get good pretzels, you can't look into the future . . . what's the advantage of being dead anyway?"

They reached the Central Park band shell, a pavilion with a large, shell-shaped stone stage in the middle. There were loads of people milling around, and darting between them were Rollerbladers and skateboarders. Some of the skateboarders were around Olivia's age, but most of them were older teenagers. She could feel Christopher's excitement as they both listened to the sound of skateboards rumbling against the pavement, the loud clap-clap as the skateboarders lifted the front edge of the boards to swivel and then slapped them down on the ground again.

When Christopher was alive he had been a daredevil skateboarder, doing tricks that Olivia bet even Barry McFarkle would envy.

Olivia knelt down, opened the duffel bag, and pulled out a skateboard.

"Jezebel!" Christopher cried out the name of his old skateboard. "What are you doing with her?"

"What do you think?" Olivia replied. She put one foot on the skateboard and rolled it back and forth, to see how it felt.

"Oooh, I don't know, Olivia . . ."

"Don't you want to take a ride on Jezebel again?" Olivia coaxed.

"Of course I do! But let's be honest, Olivia, you're not too coordinated."

It was true and Olivia knew it. But she had been planning this all week, imagining how Christopher would feel flying across pavement once again, hearing the rasp of Jezebel's wheels. She looked around at all the other kids effortlessly gliding and pivoting. If they could do it, so could she. She took a breath and began to roll along, one foot on Jezebel and the other pushing at the ground.

"Just take your time, Olivia," Christopher coached nervously. "Don't be embarrassed to stick out your arms if it helps. Oh man, I love that sound! She's still running smoothly. Now put your other foot on the board, bend your knees . . . get a feel for your balance . . . there you go!"

Suddenly Olivia was flying along, her arms spread. She could feel a rush of adrenaline from Christopher as it seeped into her own veins. It was thrilling, incredibly thrilling! She put her foot back down and pushed harder, making Jezebel fly faster, until she realized that she wasn't entirely sure how to stop. To her mortification, a boy in a beige suede hat was standing directly in her path, watching her with an amused look on his face. The look didn't change, and he didn't budge an inch, even though she was heading right for him.

"Move, you idiot!" Olivia cried, and just before she crashed into him, the boy jumped agilely out of the way, without ever losing his amused expression.

Olivia was headed straight for a lamppost. She put her arms out in front of her and at the last second leapt up and caught the lamppost in midair, wrapping her arms around it tightly. Jezebel slammed into the bottom of the lamppost, then flipped over a few times, finally resting on her back, her wheels still spinning pathetically.

"Jump down, look them all in the eye, and smile," said a quiet voice. The voice was not coming from inside her head. It was coming from the boy whom she'd nearly run down a moment before. Now he was standing in front of

her, his eyes cutting this way and that at the other kids, who were all staring at Olivia. His suede hat had a narrow brim, under which a mop of black hair was curling. He wore loose jeans and a purple T-shirt, and he was holding a skateboard under his arm. On his left elbow was a nasty black scab, and his right arm sported ugly dark scars and purple bruises, some fresh and others yellowing on the edges.

"Go on," he urged in a whisper. "They'll think you were just trying out some new trick."

Olivia glanced around. All the skateboarders were still watching her. She jumped down, and looked at them, trying hard to smile. It wasn't easy. Her chest was sore from slamming into the pole, and her ears were hot and probably bright red. But she did manage a very tiny, somewhat shaky smile. It seemed to work, because some of the skateboarders nodded approvingly, and one of them even clapped a little until his friend shoved him.

Olivia went to retrieve Jezebel, but found the boy in the beige suede hat had already picked her up and was turning her over in his hands.

"Pretty fancy skateboard," he said. He put Jezebel down, stepped on her, and pushed off.

"Hey! Who said you could ride her!" Olivia cried. The sight of some stranger on Jezebel infuriated her. The boy made a quick movement that snapped Jezebel's tail against the pavement and sent both him and Jezebel up in the air for a second before he landed again neatly. He circled back around and stopped in front of Olivia.

"This board's got some decent pop," he said, picking up Jezebel and examining her admiringly. "Maybe you should give it to someone who can actually handle it."

"Maybe you should give that stupid hat back to your grandmother," Olivia snarled, grabbing Jezebel out of his hands.

"Easy there, Killer," Christopher warned.

The boy pulled the brim of his hat down, clearly offended. He deserved it, Olivia told herself defensively.

"Not really, Olivia," Christopher said.

"I was talking to myself!" she said. She stuffed the skateboard back into her duffel bag, zipped up the bag and swung it over her shoulder, and started to stalk away from the band shell.

"I'll give you twenty bucks for that board!" the boy called after her.

"You can cram your twenty bucks!" she called back.

"Hey, forget about it, Olivia," Christopher said. "Skateboarding isn't everyone's cup of tea, you know."

"But I wanted you to ride Jezebel again," Olivia said.

"Eh, it's probably time to retire the old gal anyway. Maybe that kid was right. Maybe you should give her to someone who would really use her."

That made Olivia feel a little sick in her gut. Give up Jezebel? Jezebel was part of Christopher. For years he almost always had her with him. And underneath her, right by each wheel–the one part of the skateboard that didn't ever touch the ground and get scuffed up–were tiny blue footprints. When Olivia was five, Christopher had dipped her feet in blue paint and had her step on the bottom of his board. "That way your feet are right under mine," he'd said.

"Hey, listen, I've got to get moving. I'm supposed to put Barry McFarkle in a clothes dryer and spin him in the tumble cycle. I'll see you later, kiddo. How about Thursday? Same time?"

"Sure. . . . Christopher?"

"Hmm?"

"Do you still have to do laundry after you die?" Olivia asked.

"Why? Do you plan on taking your smelly socks into the afterlife? Take it easy, kiddo. Chin up. And about the new house . . . try not to jump to any conclusions."

It was only after he was gone that Olivia realized it was exactly what the note in her bedroom had said.

Four

On her way home Olivia passed an ice cream shop on Columbus Avenue, and she impulsively dug into her jeans pocket to see how much money she had. She extracted four crumpled dollar bills—enough for a cone.

The little ice cream shop was jammed with people. As Olivia waited in line, she peered into the glass cabinet, perusing the tubs of pastel-colored sherbets, and ice creams swirled with caramel or studded with nuts. She looked at all the names: Nutty-Butty Crunch, Creamy Coconut Droozle, Caramello-Bing Bong. In the end, however, she *always* got the same flavor: mint chocolate chip. Just thinking about it, she could practically taste the creamy tingle of the mint in her mouth and the hard snap of chocolate between her teeth. I am a creature of habit, she told herself. Nothing wrong with that.

"Can I help you?"

Olivia looked up at the boy behind the counter and opened her mouth to order, but stopped. She stared at his name tag, on which was written BRANWELL.

Branwell. The name popped out in a funny way, like a single hand waving at her in a crowd of people. She thought of Branwell, *her* Branwell, whom she had met in the last apartment building she'd lived in. Branwell was smart and kind and he was the first friend she'd made in a long time. He was also, unfortunately, dead. It was Olivia who helped him see he was a ghost, and since then she had not heard from him again, and she had missed him terribly. She had tried to contact him, the way she contacted Christopher, but there was never any response. Christopher had told her that he was probably very busy: "There's always a lot to do when you first arrive in the Spirit World. Be patient."

"Can I help you?" the boy asked again, his voice bored and a little annoyed. The voice was so different from that of the Branwell she had known, and Olivia felt yanked back into the present moment.

"Mint chocolate chip," she muttered.

"Sugar or wafer?" The boy had a permanent yawn in his voice.

"Sugar."

With a few practiced flicks, the boy scooped out a cone for Olivia, handed it to her, and took her money. As he gave her back her change, she looked at his name tag again. Odd. The boy was nothing like Branwell–not in the way he looked or acted or spoke–yet Olivia found herself reluctant to leave. She knew it was silly and sentimental, but she just wanted to be around a Branwell, even if it was the wrong Branwell.

She took a seat at one of the little round tables near the wall. She felt a dull ache in her chest where she had slammed into the pole. In her duffel bag, Jezebel rested lightly against Olivia's legs. Give Jezebel away? Olivia frowned. Christopher had never said that before. In fact, whenever they spoke, he almost always asked about Jezebel. Why would he want to give her away now? Just because Olivia had some trouble riding her? Lots of kids knew how to skateboard, so why couldn't Olivia learn too?

A surge of kids in school uniforms suddenly came into the store. Among them Olivia spotted Frannie, who caught her eye and smiled at her. The kids were accompanied by a woman with stiff blond hair cut in a pageboy style, the ends clipped razor sharp.

"No need to stand in line, children," the blond woman told the kids. "Push your way to the front, there you go!"

The children pushed to the front, producing loud protests from the people already in line.

"Never mind them!" the woman called out. "The common folk will always grumble. Dijon, you go first."

"Yes, Ms. Bender." A gangly girl of about sixteen or so, with frizzy, reddish-brown hair, stepped forward meekly, clearly embarrassed. With a thick city accent, she said to the counter girl, "Can I please have a cone of vanilla-cherry swirl? With some of dem rainbowy sprinkles?"

"Do not *order* your ice cream, Dijon!" Ms. Bender instructed. "*Demand* your ice cream!"

"Um . . . I demand a cone of vanilla-cherry swirl," Dijon said, her voice even quieter than before. "And . . . um . . . some of dem rainbowy sprinkles, please–"

"Do not say *please,* Dijon!" Ms. Bender corrected her angrily, which made Dijon even more nervous.

"I mean . . . I mean . . . gimme some vanilla-cherry swirl with dem freakin' rainbowy sprinkles!" Dijon blurted out in a shrill, panicky voice. Frannie groaned.

The girl behind the counter stared back at Dijon coldly. She was wearing a name tag that said SHELLY.

"*Excuse* me?" Shelly snarled.

"Excellent, children, we've got a live one!" Ms. Bender

exclaimed excitedly. "Now, Dijon, lift your chin, flare your nostrils, that's it!"

Poor Dijon happened to have a pair of very large, round nostrils, and when she flared them, they flapped and made a funny squeak.

Shelly lifted her upper lip disdainfully. "My brother has a guinea pig that does that."

Ms. Bender yanked Dijon back by the collar of her shirt. "You're pitiful, Dijon! That just earned you a D-minus. Wait for us outside. Melbourne, you're up next."

"Poor Dijon." Frannie had edged away from the rest of her group and was standing next to Olivia's table. "That's my sister. She's just not cut out for this. Hey, I heard a whole lot of yelling outside Ansel's house last night. What was going on?"

"I'm not sure. I—" Olivia started, but Ms. Bender yelled, "Venice! Pay attention!"

Melbourne was doing pretty well, it seemed. He was a stocky boy with a thick neck and very shiny black hair, and he naturally held his chin up very high.

"Fetch me a cone of twirley-swirley fudgie, what," Melbourne was saying to the counter girl, Shelly. "And mind, I know all your little tricks, what."

"What tricks?" Shelly narrowed her eyes at Melbourne. Most people would have shrunk from such a look, but Melbourne was unfazed.

"Scooping the ice cream so that there is a pocket of air in the middle, what."

Shelly looked at her coworker Branwell with an expression of utter disbelief. Branwell shrugged in a very boring way.

Melbourne stamped his foot. "Get me my cone, girl, chop, chop, what! Stop dillydallying."

"Out!" Shelly yelled at Melbourne, pointing at the door. "Out, before I pop you in the nose!"

"Excellent!" Ms. Bender said, looking at her watch. "Just a hair under two minutes! Well done, Melbourne."

Melbourne backed away from the counter, looking very self-satisfied.

"I don't get it," Olivia said to Frannie. "Why is everyone so happy? He was just kicked out of the store."

"That's the whole point," Frannie said miserably. "Ms. Bender says that if we are going to pass as wealthy children, we have to learn to be rude to the 'riffraff'—that means salesgirls, waiters, people like that. We've been doing this all day. So far we've been kicked out of fifteen stores on Columbus Avenue."

Olivia thought of the Princepessa Christina Lilli. She was a real princess, and she had always been very polite to Olivia's father, who would be, Olivia was pretty sure, considered riffraff.

"That doesn't seem very sensible," Olivia said.

"It's positively mortifying," Frannie whispered, right before Ms. Bender herded her outside.

Olivia popped the last morsel of cone into her mouth. She picked up the duffel bag and started to leave but turned to steal a final glimpse at Branwell. He was carefully counting out change for a lady. He must have felt her eyes on him, because he looked at her. For a second, Olivia thought she detected a sudden brightness in his eyes. But it was only for a second, and then his eyes became dull again and he turned back to his customer, his mouth lolling open in a dopey gawp.

FIVE

In the evening George and Olivia sat down to dinner in the brownstone's huge kitchen. It was the only room downstairs that wasn't under water. Nora said that it used to be, but that she got seasick when she was cooking, so Ansel had raised the floor above the water level.

Olivia and her dad were alone for the first time that day—Ansel and Nora were floating on a sofa in the lagoon, immersed in a game of gin rummy. Olivia watched her father carefully as he spooned out a square of the lasagna that Nora had made and plopped it on Olivia's plate. He had a funny, perplexed look on his face.

"So, did you work on the plumbing, Dad?" Olivia asked, trying but failing to keep the eagerness out of her voice.

"No." He plopped a piece of lasagna on his own plate, and spread his napkin on his lap.

"Fix anything?"

"Nope."

"So, what did you do?"

"Hmm. Well . . . after we went fishing, we played badminton in the backyard, and when I asked Ansel if he didn't have a room that needed painting or a floor that needed sanding, he said, 'Oh yes, yes, plenty of time for that. But right now we *must* go horseback riding in Central Park!' And now the day is finished and I haven't done any work at all. I should feel guilty, and yet . . . it was the most wonderful day I've had in ages!"

Olivia frowned. She didn't like the sound of that. She had wanted to tell him what she'd heard last night, but he seemed so happy . . . and although things had certainly sounded sinister, she wasn't *positive* . . . and Christopher had told her to use her gray matter. She decided to wait to mention it to her father, but she'd be keeping her eyes and ears open, Ansel could bet on that!

She took a bite of her lasagna. The noodles were so undercooked, they were crunchy, and the cheese was rubbery. She made a face and spit it out into her napkin.

"Oh, come on, Olivia," George said. "It's lasagna. How bad can it possibly taste?"

"I don't know, how bad does an old, crusty pencil eraser

taste?" she said. He shot her a doubtful look and took a bite. But after a valiant effort at chewing it, he spit his out in the napkin too. Then he stood up decisively, picked up his and Olivia's plates, and slid their contents into the garbage.

"How about a little Spy and Fry?" he said, and he raised his eyebrows up and down.

"Do you think Ansel will mind?" Olivia asked.

"He told me to help myself to anything in the kitchen. Go on, Olivia, you spy."

She jumped out of her seat and flung open all the cabinet doors and opened the refrigerator. She loved Spy and Fry. She and her father used to do it whenever they couldn't think of anything to make for dinner. Olivia would spy out different ingredients lying around the house, and George would find a way to combine them and make them into something delicious. Sometimes she'd deliberately choose things that didn't seem like they went together. But George was a regular magician with food, and no matter what she chose, he would whip up something that tasted fabulous.

Olivia stood on a chair and pulled things out of the cabinet–a bag of tortilla chips, a bag of marshmallows, a can of almonds, and cayenne pepper–and then out of the fridge—a chicken breast, a strange greenish fruit that Olivia had never seen before, an onion, ketchup, and three eggs. George looked at all the ingredients in front of him. He moved them around, as if he were trying to decide what went with what, his face tight with concentration.

"Challenging, challenging," he mused. "But not impossible." Then he nodded slowly and said, "Okay, let's start chopping!"

Olivia began chopping an onion and George was peeling the greenish fruit, and it was all so pleasant and familiar that Olivia forgot how much she hated the house. Her mind drifted and George was humming something tuneless, when suddenly he stopped and looked over at Olivia.

"You know, I bet Christopher would have really liked Ansel. He's just so . . ." George searched for the right word. Olivia held her breath, hoping he wouldn't say it, but he did. *". . . charming,"* George said.

That night Olivia lay awake in bed, listening, a nervous current skittering through her body. Off in the distance she could hear the traffic humming along the avenues, but the sound was muffled. In fact, the house was strangely quiet, Olivia thought. It was as though the entire brownstone were submerged in water, not just the first floor, and all the sounds of the city above it were smothered.

The thick silence was lulling, and although she resisted, Olivia gradually drifted off to sleep. She awoke only once during the night, to hear a ferocious growling and bellowing from the floor below, then silence. A moment later she heard the applause of many hands.

In the morning, after she showered and dressed, she grabbed Jezebel. She would practice with her every day, and by the time Thursday rolled around, she'd be able to give Christopher a real surprise.

Outside, she spotted Frannie crossing the street, dressed in a smart little summer dress rather than her uniform, walking jauntily toward the school. Olivia's first thought was that such a tiny kid shouldn't be crossing the street by herself. Then she remembered that Frannie was really fourteen.

"Howdy," Frannie said cheerfully.

"Hi. How come you're not in your uniform?"

"I just came back from a visit with my mom. Actually, it was kind of an important visit . . . it was the first time I met Claude, and Claude introduced both me and Mom to his father."

"How'd it go?" Olivia asked.

"Not great, but I guess it could have been worse. Claude's father, Mr. Vondychomps, asked us all kinds of questions–about our ancestors and our finances–and poor Mom didn't do too well, but I stuck in a bunch of talk about my pony and how I loved the Dover sole at Balthazar restaurant. Later, when I was looking for the bathroom, I overheard Mr. Vondychomps and Claude in the study, arguing about my mother. Mr. Vondychomps said, 'She's what I call a snow globe, son. You know what that is, don't you? It's a glass globe with snow inside that you shake up to amuse yourself. Yes, a snow globe–very pretty and completely useless.' Well, I got so mad. I mean, it's sort of true. But honestly, what a snobby thing to say. So I couldn't help myself, and I said, 'Actually, a snow globe does have a use. It makes for a very valuable paperweight.' I thought he'd be furious at me for eavesdropping, and I think he almost was. But then he laughed a little, and said he'd always wanted a clever child–which made Claude go all red in the face. Then he opened his desk with a key and took something out.

" 'Now, *this* is a valuable paperweight,' he said. 'And I am giving it to you as a present. For sticking up for your mother.' It was a pretty cool-looking paperweight. And I can see his objections to my mom. But frankly, Claude's even dumber than she is, so they make a pretty good match. We just have to convince Mr. Vondychomps of that, because if he tells Claude not to marry Mom, he won't marry her. Claude's devoted to his father, does everything he tells him to do."

"What happens if Claude doesn't marry your mother?"

"That would be a pure disaster!" Frannie cried.

"Why?"

"Well, think about it. Ms. Bender's school isn't cheap, you know. My mom sold everything she owned to get us in here. It's sort of like betting all your money on a horse at the racetrack. So Dijon and I have got to try and run a little faster, you know what I mean? I'd better go in. I've got a test in an hour on ordering room service in hotels."

Olivia headed for Central Park. It felt nice to hold Jezebel beneath her arm. It made her feel like a normal kid. When people see me, she thought, they'll just think I'm off to hang out with my friends, and that we're all going to skateboard for a while, and then maybe we'll go see a movie, or go to someone's house and talk about the kids we don't like and play CDs and . . . She lost herself in this daydream until she saw two girls coming up the street. They were talking and laughing, and all of a sudden Olivia remembered who she really was: Olivia Kidney—the girl who was always the strange new kid. The girl who no one ever wanted to talk to, if they even noticed her at all.

That thought put her in a foul mood. She hugged Jezebel close to her side. Well, she had Christopher, anyway. And he was better—much, much, much better—than any French-braiding, boy-crazy, fingernail-filing, blathering idiot girls her own age. And now she could help Christopher in ways that she never could when he was alive. She could make him feel the excitement of shooting along the street on Jezebel, and maybe, eventually, she could do some fancy tricks. *Nobody* else could do that for Christopher. In fact, she mused, he needed her now even more than he did when he was alive.

At the Delacorte Theater her eye drifted once more to the statue of Romeo and Juliet. She stopped and gazed up at Juliet's smooth bronze arm wrapped around Romeo's neck.

Close behind her came a loud and haughty sniff, then a demure sneeze.

"Bless you," Olivia said. She almost never said "Bless you" to people who sneezed, since it always seemed very phony, but this was such a prim ladylike sneeze that it was almost impossible to say nothing at all.

"I hardly think you are qualified to bless me, Olivia Kidney, unless you've been ordained as a priest since I've last seen you."

Olivia whipped around at the sound of the cranky but familiar voice, and cried out, "Princepessa Christina Lilli!"

"Hush!" The Princepessa glanced around her nervously, then dabbed at her nose with a tissue. "I'd thank you not to use my title in public," she said severely. "Just 'Christina Lilli' will do." The old lady scrutinized Olivia for a moment. "You've grown," she accused Olivia. "You're threatening to become a *tall* girl."

"But I just saw you last week," Olivia protested.

"One can grow in the space of an afternoon, if one is pigheaded enough." The Princepessa sneezed again and Olivia almost said, "Bless you," but caught herself in time.

"Are you sick?" Olivia asked.

"I'm allergic to the trees," the Princepessa said.

"Then why are you in Central Park? It's full of trees."

"Because I refuse to be bullied by vegetation. Now, come away from this abominable statue." She hooked her skinny arm through Olivia's and tried to pull her away. But Olivia did not like to be bullied either.

"I don't think it's so bad," Olivia said, pulling her arm out of the Princepessa's grasp.

"That's because you don't know any better," said the Princepessa disdainfully. She tipped up her head, pressed her lips together, and blinked rapidly several times.

"As a matter of fact," Olivia said, growing annoyed now, "I think it's a really terrific statue. I think maybe it's the best statue I've ever seen." Olivia had folded her arms stubbornly across her chest. She hated to be told what she should and shouldn't like.

"Nonsense!" the Princepessa replied. "No one wants to see people kissing in public."

"They're not kissing, they're *almost* kissing. And anyway, *I* don't mind people kissing in public," Olivia claimed, which was really a lie. She didn't like to see people kissing in public either. It always seemed a sort of show-offy thing to do. But Olivia was in a contrary mood, and she was prepared to lie about any number of things, just to be disagreeable.

"That's just the sort of thing a *tall* girl would say," the Princepessa snapped, as if greatly offended. "Regards to your father," she said coldly, and she left very quickly, her little white heels clicking at the ground.

Olivia watched her go, feeling both angry at the old woman and angry at herself for being so quarrelsome. She hitched Jezebel up under her arm and followed the paved bike path, where Rollerbladers and bikers in bright spandex pants careened crazily past the slow-moving carriage horses, until she finally reached the band shell. The skateboarders were there, sure enough–lots of them. They had set up makeshift ramps out of slabs of wood and were taking turns on them. She saw the boy in the beige hat, whizzing over the ramps with some of the older boys, and she turned her head, hoping he hadn't noticed her.

Olivia walked a few yards away, to a quieter section. No one was around, except for a homeless man curled up on the bench with his back to her, sleeping. Olivia put Jezebel down on the pavement and placed her left foot on her. She pushed gently with her right foot, trying to feel the balance that Christopher had talked about. It took a while, but gradually she began to feel more steady, and even when she fell (which she did quite a bit), she was prepared for it and it didn't hurt too much. She had become so engrossed in practicing that she didn't see the boy in the suede hat until he was right in front of her. He stamped a foot on Jezebel to stop her and simultaneously grabbed Olivia around her waist to keep her from toppling as she jumped off Jezebel.

"Hands off me, creep!" Olivia cried, steadying herself, then shoving the boy away.

"Give me your board," he demanded in an urgent tone.

"Get stuffed!" Olivia replied, and she bent down to grab Jezebel. But the boy was too quick for her, and he snatched Jezebel up in his arms and ran. Olivia chased after him across the pavilion and up the steps along the side of the band shell, where he stopped suddenly and pitched Jezebel into a thick patch of bushes.

"How dare you—" Olivia cried. She started for the bushes to fish out Jezebel, but the boy in the suede hat grabbed her arm.

"Open your eyes, why don't you." He pointed back to the main pavilion, across which half a dozen police officers were now walking very purposefully toward them.

"So?" Olivia said.

"So, skateboarding is illegal in Central Park. They can confiscate your board if they catch you. Look around—notice anything?"

It took her a moment to see. Then she said, "All the other skateboarders are gone." Even the makeshift ramp had been swiftly dismantled and now was just a pile of lumber on the ground.

"Bravo, genius."

Olivia frowned. Branwell would never have spoken to her like that. "Just keep your paws off my board, okay?" she said.

"Fine." He looked at her for a minute, picking at the scab on his elbow. "My name's Ruben." He waited for Olivia to say her name, which she did, reluctantly.

"So," Ruben said, "how come you're always alone?"

"I prefer my own company," Olivia said stiffly.

"Translation: 'I have no friends.' "

It was true, and it hurt her feelings. She turned away from him so he wouldn't see her face, and saw the police officers walk past them and converge on the homeless man on the bench. One of the officers leaned over and nudged the man's shoulder.

Olivia frowned. "Why don't they just leave him alone?" she said out loud, but to herself. "It's not like he's bothering anyone."

Ruben turned and watched the police officers keenly. "It doesn't take six cops to wake up a drunk," he said after a few moments, and he started down the stairs quickly. Olivia paused, loathe to leave Jezebel in the bushes. Still, she supposed Jezebel was safe enough for the time being, and besides, she was as curious as Ruben. She followed him down the steps, and over to where the cops were prodding the homeless man. By now a small crowd had gathered, and one of the cops was talking on his radio.

"All right, folks, move along. Nothing to see," one of the

cops said, waving a hand at the crowd. But as all New Yorkers know, when cops say there is nothing to see, it means there is most definitely something to see, and no one made a move.

"Is he dead?" a woman wearing Rollerblades asked the cop. The cop ignored her, and since the homeless man's face was turned away from them, it was hard to tell.

The wail of an ambulance now could be heard growing louder and louder, and it finally appeared, making its way through the pavilion with its lights flashing. It stopped in front of the crowd, and two paramedics dressed in dark blue uniforms stepped out. They walked up to the man on the bench and gently turned him on his back. His hand dropped limply off the edge of the bench. His face was now visible. Olivia gasped. It was the red-haired man she had seen the other night–she was sure of it.

Ruben looked at her. "What's the matter?"

One of the paramedics picked up the man's wrist to check his pulse. A man in the crowd said, "Oh, he's dead all right. I already checked. I was the one who called the cops."

It was then that Olivia turned and began to walk away quickly.

"Are you going to hurl?" Ruben asked, running to catch up with her.

"Leave me alone," Olivia said. She glanced back quickly. The paramedics had lifted the man onto a stretcher and were putting him into the ambulance.

"Where are you going?" Ruben asked. When Olivia didn't answer, he repeated the question.

"To get Jezebel," she muttered distractedly.

"Who's she?" Ruben asked.

"My board." She wanted him to leave her alone. She needed to think; she needed to figure out what she should do.

"*Jezebel?* Sounds like a cow's name," Ruben said.

"And Ruben sounds like the name of a dumb redneck!" Olivia retorted. Ruben's face grew very pink at this, and he stopped following her.

"Come on, Olivia, that's not fair. Go back and say you're sorry." She heard the voice in her head, and for a moment she thought Christopher was with her. But then she realized it was just her own thoughts, giving her advice. Advice she decided to completely ignore.

Six

On her walk back to the brownstone Olivia turned the problem over and over in her mind. She *had* to tell her father. She was using her gray matter, and her gray matter was telling her that Ansel had done something to cause that man's death. She was sure of it.

When she got back to the brownstone, it appeared that everyone was out. She rowed herself to the stairs, ran up to the fourth floor, and looked in her father's room—empty. She went to her own room to put Jezebel under the bed. Her right forearm was scraped up pretty badly, and her left hand had a cut. In all the excitement at the band shell, she hadn't even noticed. She went into the bathroom and washed off her wounds. Then she opened up the medicine cabinet. There was nothing in there but a bottle of pills, which had expired in 1979, a bottle of calamine lotion, and rubbing alcohol.

Olivia opened the bottle of rubbing alcohol and poured it over her forearm and hand, wincing at the sting but feeling a tiny swell of pride at her injuries.

"These?" she imagined saying to her friends. "Oh, they're nothing. Just a few skateboard injuries." She liked the sound of that. But though the injuries were real enough, the friends were only imaginary. She thrust aside this thought–there were more important things to worry about at the moment. She recapped the alcohol and headed back downstairs to find her father.

She rowed through the canal, looking in all the rooms. As she came to the kitchen, she saw Nora vigorously shaking salt on hamburger patties. Olivia stopped rowing and grabbed on to the wall of the kitchen entrance to keep the boat steady.

"Have you seen my father?" Olivia asked.

"He's out," Nora said without pausing in her salt shaking. "He and Ansel are marching in the Fireman's Parade."

"Ansel's a fireman?" Olivia asked.

"Nah, he just likes a good parade."

A timer rang and Nora said, "Lucky you, kid, you're just in time." Nora yanked opened the oven door and pulled out a pie. The edges of the pie were prettily crimped and a nice, toasty brown color, but a greenish-red juice was oozing out of little slits across the top crust.

"Hang on, I'll cut you a slice."

Olivia eyed the pie warily. "What kind of pie is it?"

"Well, I'm not completely sure," Nora said, cutting a hefty wedge and slopping it onto a plate. "I picked the berries from a bush in the garden."

"How do you know they're not poisonous?" Olivia asked.

"I don't," Nora said, placing a fork on the plate. She walked over to the boat and leaned down to hand the plate to Olivia. "But life is full of risks, hey?"

"Thanks, I'll pass," Olivia said, waving the plate away. Nora sniffed the air, then narrowed her eyes at Olivia. She put the plate of pie down on the floor, then stepped right into the boat. She sat down opposite Olivia and looked at her with stern green eyes, then pointed a blue-polished fingernail at Olivia's nose. "Now once and for all, I'm telling you this for your own good, kid: LAY OFF THE HOOCH!"

"What?" Olivia asked.

"You've been drinking again! And don't even bother to lie to me, because I can smell it on you."

This baffled Olivia for a moment until she realized what Nora was smelling.

"It's rubbing alcohol–" Olivia started to explain.

"Alcohol is alcohol, kid." Nora waved Olivia's explanation away. Her face softened a little and she said, "Look, I'm not judging you or anything. I'm no angel myself. I used to be as wild as they come, stealing cars, going out till all hours of the night, drinking and raising hell. It's amazing I survived those years." She sighed and shook her head, remembering. "It was Ansel who saved me, you know. He found me on his doorstep one evening in bad shape. He took me in—no questions asked. He's the kindest man in the world."

"I doubt that," Olivia couldn't help saying. Nora raised her eyebrows.

"Boy, you're one of those angry drunks, aren't you?"

"I'm just saying that he may not be as nice as you think he is."

"Oh yeah?" Nora eyed Olivia suspiciously. "Why?"

Olivia bit her lip. It was stupid of her to let that slip out.

"Like . . . ," Olivia stammered, trying to think up something quickly, "like . . . like the fact that he makes you work like a dog—rowing him all around the house and cleaning and cooking, while he goes out marching in parades!"

"I don't like parades." Nora shrugged. There was a pause before she added, "And anyway, I *never* go outside."

For the first time in their conversation Nora's eyes shifted away from Olivia's.

"Never? You must go out sometimes," Olivia said.

"Nope."

"You mean he keeps you in here? Like a prisoner!?" Olivia cried.

"Don't be such a drama queen. Of course he doesn't *keep* me in here. I have what they call agoraphobia. Which means I have a fear of going outside. Whenever I stay outside for more than a few minutes, my heart starts pounding in my chest and I can barely breathe, and I have to run back inside before I pass out. It just started this past year, but frankly it's probably for the best anyway. Staying inside keeps me out of trouble."

"I bet Ansel told you that, didn't he?" Olivia said angrily. She was really beginning to hate Ansel now.

"Well, it's the truth, kid. And here's some more truth—unless you quit your boozing, you're headed for an unhappy end."

The phone rang, and Nora stood up and leapt off the boat to answer it in the kitchen, making the boat rock wildly. Olivia stiffened up and held her breath—this was nearly as bad as being in an elevator! When the rocking eased, she lifted her oar and was about to use it to push the boat away from the kitchen, when she saw that Nora was walking back toward her with the phone.

"It's for you," Nora said. "A Miss Kissingly. She sounds like a real cranky old fossil."

"I can hear you, young lady!" came the voice from the telephone.

It was the Princepessa. Olivia took the phone out of Nora's hands.

"Hi, Pri–Christina Lilli," Olivia said.

"No wonder you're going from bad to worse, if that's the company you're keeping," the Princepessa said tartly. "Now tell me . . . have you any clothing that does not involve stained T-shirts, denim, or sneakers that smell like wet dog?"

Olivia thought for a moment. "No," she concluded.

"Nonsense, child, you must own a dress."

Actually, Olivia did own one dress. Her mother had sent it to her for Olivia's twelfth birthday, along with a card that said, *Happy Eleventh Birthday to the Daughter I Cherish!*

"Okay, I guess I do have one," Olivia admitted.

"Good. Go and put it on. We are going out to dine."

"Thanks anyway," Olivia said, "but I think I'm going to wait for my dad to come home."

"Oh, I wouldn't bother," Nora said, eavesdropping.

"Ansel and your father won't be home till late. After the parade, they're going salsa dancing."

Olivia thought for a second. It was useless to stay home and brood. And besides, she felt sort of guilty about the way she'd behaved with the Princepessa.

"All right," Olivia said. "I'll go."

"Of course you will. And comb your hair or I'll comb it for you."

Seven

After she showered, Olivia fished out the birthday dress from her closet. It was a knee-length lavender dress with a scoop collar, and it fit surprisingly well. Olivia looked at herself in the ornately framed full-length mirror hanging on the wall. Maybe she *had* gotten taller. She thought of tall girls she'd known. Mostly they reminded Olivia of floor lamps. But then she thought of Bineta, one of Christopher's old girlfriends. She was from Senegal, Africa, and she was six feet, one inch tall. But she walked with her chin up and her broad shoulders thrown back, and Christopher had said she was "a goddess in the flesh, no kidding."

Olivia pushed her chin up and her shoulders back. If she was going to be tall, she might as well be tall like Bineta.

She supposed that the Princepessa was planning on taking her out to a fancy restaurant. Olivia had never been to a fancy restaurant. She imagined that the waiters would wear black ties and put cloth napkins on your lap. And that, at the end of the meal, a dessert cart would be wheeled up to the table, crammed full of pastries and frosted cakes and pies (and not the kind made of potentially poisonous berries!). Olivia's mouth began to water, and her stomach rumbled in anticipation.

She hurried back downstairs, where she heard the splash, splash of oars–Nora gliding up the canal. Sitting behind her, very erect and with her handbag on her lap, was the Princepessa. She was dressed in a floor-length black-beaded gown.

"Well, your friend's quite the sailor!" Nora told Olivia happily. "We nearly collided with the bathtub, but your friend grabbed up the spare oar and helped steer us around."

The Princepessa waved off the compliment, but Olivia could tell she was pleased. It made Olivia happy to see the Princepessa in a good mood. Even though she was persnickety and exasperating, Olivia was really very fond of her.

"Well," the Princepessa said, looking up and down at Olivia's dress, "I suppose it will have to do. In any case, I've brought a few gewgaws to make you more presentable. Come, come, child, step aboard."

Olivia stepped into the boat and sat down. The Princepessa reached into a large paper bag on the floor beside her and pulled out a diamond tiara (which was a little half crown, the kind they put on Miss America's head when she wins) and a brown fur wrap with a gold clasp, to be worn around your shoulders.

"Put them on, child," the Princepessa commanded. Olivia looked at the ridiculous items, then glanced over at Nora, whose eyes were wide with amusement.

"But I'll look like a weirdo," Olivia protested. The Princepessa's lips compressed with displeasure. Olivia sighed. She placed the tiara on her head and fastened the wrap around her shoulders. Nora laughed out loud, then muttered "Sorry" to the Princepessa.

"You look lovely," the Princepessa declared firmly.

Nora let them out at the lagoon landing, where the Princepessa hitched up her gown and deftly stepped onto the marble walkway.

"Tell my dad to wait up for me, okay?" Olivia said to Nora. "I need to talk to him. It's really important."

"Sure, sure, I'll tell him. And hey . . . give 'em hell, ladies, woop-woop!!" Nora stuck her oar straight up in the air.

"Spirited young lady," the Princepessa said. Then she sniffed. "Not a bad sort though."

"She's all right," Olivia agreed. As they walked out the front door, Olivia crossed her fingers that Frannie wouldn't see her in this getup. She looked around—no Frannie, thank heavens. Still, as they walked down to Broadway, people stared at them openly, and some actually giggled.

"Where's the restaurant?" Olivia asked anxiously.

"Not far," the Princepessa replied vaguely. They walked block after block with no sign of stopping. For an old lady, the Princepessa could walk very fast, and Olivia had to practically jog to keep up with her.

"Nearly there," the Princepessa assured her several times.

Finally the Princepessa came to an abrupt halt and said, "This is it." They were standing in front of a store with a dented blue sign above the door that said, Here Hair. In the store's grimy, streaked window was a display of very small wigs on very small Styrofoam heads. The wigs were done up in elaborate fashions—some of them piled high in coils of thick braids woven through with ribbons, others with long ringlets or with great pouffy bangs. There were even men's wigs with long sideburns. But they were all too small to fit on a normal-sized person's head.

"I thought you said we were going to dinner," Olivia protested. Her stomach was burning, she was so hungry.

"Fix your tiara, it's crooked," the Princepessa said, and she opened the door.

Inside, the store was very narrow, but it stretched far back, its walls lined with shelves of more miniature wigs on little Styrofoam heads. It looked like hundreds of dolls had had their heads cut off. In the back of the store, sitting on a stool, was a buxom woman on whose lap was sitting a squalling baby wearing a brown wig. The wig swirled around the baby's head in a towering updo that resembled a chocolate wedding cake, smothered with pink and green ribbons. The wig was being adjusted by a very ominous-looking man wearing a curious round hat, shaped like the lid of a mustard jar, and a loose purple shirt belted by a red sash and billowing over purple trousers. His gray hair was thick and reached halfway down his back, and he had a very menacing-looking scar on his face that started below his right eye and snaked down to his upper lip, which it pulled up into a permanent sneer. A cigarette dangled from the other side of his mouth.

"Well," the woman said, examining her child, "it's a beautiful wig, of course, but the price is rather high . . ."

The man was silent for a moment, which made the woman squirm a little on the stool. Then he removed the cigarette from between his lips, blew out a slow stream of smoke, and said, "Wigs made of human hair are costly, *madam*." He said *madam* the way other people say *moron*. "But if you would prefer a *synthetic* wig for your baby, I can show you what we have." He went to the shelves and snatched a wig off its foam head. It was bright orange with two thick, coarse braids. He held the wig out to her by one of its braids, as if it were a rat he had caught.

"This might be more suitable for you," he said. His sneering lip lifted even higher, revealing very white wolfish teeth. "It's synthetic and *cheap,* madam. Of course, it may irritate your baby's scalp. Nothing serious, just a little redness and pus-filled blisters. And take care not to hold the baby while you are cooking, as the wig has a tendency to catch fire . . ."

The woman's face grew pale and she stood up rather quickly, clutching her baby close, and said, "No, no, the wig she has on will do just fine." She reached into her bag and handed the man several bills, which he counted out slowly and carefully.

"Excellent choice, madam. Shall I wrap it for you?"

"No, she'll wear it out." And the woman carried her bewigged and crying baby past Olivia and the Princepessa, and out the door.

Olivia snorted. "A baby in a wig! That's the most ridiculous thing I've ever seen! What kind of person would make their baby wear a wig?"

"Any self-respecting Babatavian parent, that's who," the Princepessa replied.

"Baba–who?" Olivia asked. "Oh, right. That's the country you came from, isn't it?"

"It's the country I *ruled,* young lady. And wigging your baby is an ancient tradition, tracing all the way back to the Middle Ages, when the Black Plague swept through Europe. People were dying by the thousands all around us, but the Babatavians never grew sick. No one knew why . . . until it was discovered that people who wore wigs made with Babatavian hair also stayed healthy. It was our hair—which has always been prized for its thickness and luster—that repelled the disease."

Olivia twisted her lips skeptically. "That doesn't sound too scientific to me. And besides, no one gets the Black Plague anymore."

The scarred man came up to them then, his cigarette waggling between his lips. Instinctively, Olivia shrank back, but the Princepessa nodded at him familiarly.

"Good evening, Drozlop," she said. "I'm here to dine."

The man took a drag on his cigarette, then blew the smoke out slowly as he eyed Olivia with suspicion.

"What about *her?*" he asked the Princepessa, nodding toward Olivia.

"She's my guest," the Princepessa said firmly.

The man clearly was not happy about this, but after sneering at Olivia for a few seconds, he turned without a word and led them toward the back of the shop. He stopped in front of the shelf on the left wall, grabbed hold of the edge of it, and with some effort slid it to one side, making the Styrofoam heads jiggle. Behind it was a steep staircase going down into darkness. Floating up from below, Olivia could hear the sound of slow, mournful music.

The Princepessa thanked the scarred man and they started down the dark stairway, which was filled with a strange smell–sort of like the smell of the ocean after someone had poured spices into it. The Princepessa knocked on the door at the bottom of the stairs. It had a sign on it saying BEWARE. HIGH VOLTAGE. DO NOT ENTER.

The door was opened by a man with thick, wavy red-gold hair that reached his hips. He wore the same strange round cap as the man upstairs, and over his black shirt and pants he wore a colorfully embroidered vest.

"Welcome, ladies," he said. "A table for two?"

This was definitely not the sort of restaurant that Olivia was expecting. There were no white tablecloths and waiters with black ties. Instead, the customers were sitting on cushions on the carpeted floor around low copper tables crammed with clay pots.

Most of the men were wearing round caps and colorful billowy shirts, and many of the women wore ankle-length dresses topped with tunics, beneath which they wore white blouses with intricate embroidery down the sleeves. Everyone looked up when the Princepessa opened the door, their eyes strangely hopeful. Then they turned back to their food with forlorn, disappointed faces.

The waiter led them to a table in the corner, and Olivia watched the Princepessa hitch up her gown and sit cross-legged on the floor. Olivia did the same, then looked around.

"What is this place?" Olivia asked. The walls were covered with blue-and-orange tiles, and in the opposite corner of the room three men were blowing into bamboo flutes, creating the most hauntingly sad music Olivia had ever heard.

"The Babatavian Café," replied the Princepessa proudly. "It's the only Babatavian restaurant in New York, and you're privileged to be here. They don't usually allow foreigners."

"The customers don't look like they're having a very good time," Olivia said, staring around at the solemn faces.

"They don't come here for a good time. They come here in the hopes of finding what they're seeking. And most of them will be disappointed."

"What are they seeking?" Olivia asked.

"Loved ones. Their children, their husbands, their wives . . . Ah, the Babatavian Revolution was long and bloody, and families were torn apart, or worse. Children were ripped from their mother's arms, husbands were taken to prisons, wives were forced to flee to other parts of the world. It was a terrible time . . ." The Princepessa shook her head and looked around at the other customers. "But Babatavians are an optimistic people. They come here in hopes of being reunited with those long-lost loved ones. Sometimes it happens. Then there are tears and singing and glasses of wine passed around the restaurant, and there is no happier place in all of New York City. But most nights it is like this. Disappointed faces. Still, each time the door opens, there is always hope."

The man with the long red-gold hair returned, carrying a tremendous tray laden with clay pots of various sizes. He began to place them on the table, and Olivia saw that they were filled with food, most of it strange and unrecognizable.

"But we didn't order yet," Olivia protested.

"No one orders here," the Princepessa said.

"But what if I don't like it?" Olivia asked, staring dubiously at a bowl of something that looked like burnt golf balls.

The waiter raised his eyebrows at this, and the Princepessa said, "You'll have to excuse her. She has the manners of an orangutan. She's not Babatavian, you see."

"Ahh." The waiter nodded pityingly, then poured tea into each of their cups and left.

Olivia looked at the strange food. Although it didn't look particularly appetizing, it sure smelled good.

"They forgot to give me silverware," Olivia said after she had searched the table for it.

"No need." The Princepessa picked up a chunk of meat in her hands and began to gnaw at it.

"Ha! And *I* have the manners of an orangutan," Olivia muttered.

"It's a Babatavian custom to eat with your hands. Try one of these." She picked up one of the black golf balls and deposited it on Olivia's plate. Olivia frowned down at it. After a moment, she picked it up and bit into it. It made her lips pucker up, but then it tasted sugary, then puckery again.

"What is it?" she asked.

"A dried lemon rolled in sugar. Do you like it?"

Olivia took another bite and shook her head no, then nodded. It was really hard to tell. But she also couldn't stop eating it. She tried everything else too, and none of it tasted like anything she'd ever eaten before. There were meats with strange spices that tasted like flowers, and there were pickled vegetables, and pastries filled with beans, and the tea, which smelled a little bit like wet dirt, actually tasted like apples. Olivia ate until her belly ached. Then she leaned back against the cushion and sighed contentedly, watching the Princepessa stuff handfuls of rice into her mouth.

The waiter returned several times to refill their tea, and each time the Princepessa smiled and thanked him graciously. Olivia thought of the kids at Ms. Bender's School for Superior Children, and how they were instructed to be rude to waiters. And here was a real, actual princess being perfectly polite to the waiter. They should take a few lessons from the Princepessa, Olivia thought.

"Hey," Olivia suddenly leaned across the table and whispered, "don't the people here know you're the Princepessa?"

The Princepessa finished chewing, then wiped her mouth with the back of her hand.

"No," she said. "I was quite young when I left Babatavia, during the Revolution. They would not know me. And I prefer it that way. I come here every night at five o'clock for the same reason everyone else does: to find someone."

The music had grown livelier and three fat women with brightly colored silk veils wrapped around their bodies came out and began to dance around the restaurant. They jiggled their jiggly bodies to the music, and some of the customers cheered up and began to clap in time.

"Who are you trying to find?" Olivia asked.

"No one of consequence. Just a boy—well, he would be a man now, and quite an old one, but in my mind he is always a boy."

"What's his name?" Olivia asked.

The Princepessa wrapped her narrow fingers around her cup of tea and sighed. "I'll tell you a story," she said.

Eight

"When I was a young girl," the Princepessa began, "I was quite ignorant of the outside world. It came from being a princess, of course. I was coddled, and indulged, and pampered, and everyone was careful that I should not see or experience a single unpleasant thing. In my country, a Princepessa's tears were considered more valuable than any jewels, partly because of a strange genetic quirk in the Royal Family. The women in the Royal Family have very tiny tear ducts (they also have only four toes on each foot, but that has nothing to do with this story), and after the age of two, we have only one really good cry left in us. And since our tears were used as a dowry for our marriage, a Princepessa was not allowed to cry after the age of two, right up until her wedding day. On that day her husband-to-be would pinch her until she cried, and the tears were collected in a vial and put in a vault that was guarded round the clock. If a girl over two years old was caught crying, word of it would inevitably get around, and none of the princes would marry her since she had very likely shed all her priceless tears.

"Consequently, the palace was very careful about keeping me happy. The grass on the palace grounds was always perfectly clipped, and a man was hired to pluck out the earthworms and ants with a pair of tweezers so that I would never have to see such things. When I was naughty, the Royal Spanker would not spank me, but would instead spank a girl named Klotchya, who wailed and sobbed in the most satisfactory way. Even when I developed a zit, the Royal Dermatologist would creep in while I was sleeping and squeeze it so slowly and gently that I never even awoke–well, only once, and he told me he thought I was so adorable that he felt compelled to pinch my cheek. I had him thrown in prison for that, and it was only many years later that I realized what he was doing, but by the time they released him, he was quite insane. He was under the delusion that he was a woman's handbag and was constantly spitting coins out of his mouth.

"So of course I was unaware that the villagers outside the palace were, most of them, hungry and poor and generally in a foul mood. There was talk of a rebellion, and the Royal Advisers began to worry. They called a meeting and came up with a plan. They would hold a lottery each year.

They would put the names of all the village children in a hat, and whichever child was chosen would be taken in to the Royal Palace, dressed in silks and draped in jewels, and educated to become a noble lady or gentleman. Well, this did make the villagers much less grumpy, since they could now live in the slim hope that it would be their child who would be chosen.

"I remember quite well the first child who won the lottery. He was a filthy little brat, but they scrubbed him and cut his toenails and scraped out his ears and dressed him in fine silks. But he said that the silks felt like the skin of a worm, and he refused to wear them. Instead, he ran around the palace completely naked, did his lessons naked, ate his dinner naked, rode his pony naked. It was very unpleasant for all of us. They finally sent him off to a boarding school in Sweden, and we never saw him again.

"After that fiasco, the Royal Advisers were far more careful. They searched the town for the runtiest, sickliest child—the sort of child who looked like he wouldn't last through the winter—and when they held the lottery, they put glue on the paper containing the child's name, so that it would stick to the King's fingers as he pulled out the winner.

"It was a scheme that worked quite well for a while. The first sickly child stayed alive for a mere month in the castle, and when the Royal Advisers told his parents about his death, they were not at all surprised. The second child was a sallow-faced girl who coughed when she wasn't crying, and sneezed when she wasn't coughing, and cried when she wasn't sneezing. One day, she did all three at the same time, and expired on the spot.

"But the third child . . . the third child was a problem.

"I was about ten when he first arrived. His family lived in a cave way up in the hills on the outskirts of town. In fact, his ancestors had lived in that very same cave for thousands of years, all the way back to prehistoric times. There were cave paintings on the walls painted by his great-great-great-great- (don't make me go on, you get the picture) grandfather, who was a gifted caveman artist. Although his paintings were of the typical caveman subjects—fierce woolly mammoths and saber-toothed tigers being hunted by cavemen holding spears—all the animals in his paintings were wearing big, toothy, goofy smiles. He had painted them this way so as not to scare the little children who slept in the cave.

"The cave family had many children, all of them short, square, and robust, with faces that looked like prizefighters who had lost too many fights. Except for one son, who was about eleven years old. He was frail and small, and he had a limp because he suffered from rickets.

" 'He's deliciously decrepit-looking!' exclaimed one of the Royal Advisers when they found him. 'He can't have but a few months more of life left in him.'

"So the glue was put on the paper with his name on it (actually he had no name that they could discern, since his family communicated by a series of grunts and whoops, which they themselves all understood quite well. So the Advisers simply wrote *the caveboy*), and the paper stuck to the Royal Fingers and the caveboy was selected.

"When they came to take the limping, sickly caveboy to the castle, his mother grunted and whooped and squealed most forcefully (in fact, she was saying, 'Please do not take my beloved Gleechweeehunk. He is the joy of my humble existence and he has a superior mind that you all, who are so clearly barbaric and stupid, could not possibly appreciate.'). But the Advisers ignored the woman and hauled the boy off in the Royal Carriage.

"I remember when I first laid eyes on him. It was in the morning, when I came out of my bedchamber, and I tripped on him. He was lying outside the door of my bedchamber in a heap. They had dressed him in silks, but he had wrapped himself in the musty old bearskin that he wore in the cave, so I thought I had tripped on a dead animal. I screamed and screamed until the servants came running and hustled him away.

"He had his own room–a perfectly fine room–but he always slept outside my bedchamber. Perhaps it was because my bedchamber was at the darker end of a very long hall with a vaulted ceiling, which might have reminded him of being back in his family's cave. But who knows. He was a strange boy. Still, I grew used to him sleeping there, and I simply stepped right on him when I left my bedchamber in the morning. Thus, I began to call him 'The Thing That I Step On.'

" 'Your back is too bony,' I told him one morning after I had trod upon him in my slippers. 'It makes the soles of my feet ache when I walk on it.'

"So The Thing That I Step On began to eat more, and little by little he began to put on weight.

" 'Your arms are too weak,' I told him on another occasion. 'See how you wince when I dig my heels into your biceps? I don't like to see a wincing face first thing in the morning–it puts me off my oatmeal.'

"So The Thing That I Step On began to exercise. He

spent the days out in the Royal Forest lifting tree stumps and swimming through the pond, and little by little he began to grow stronger.

" 'When I step on you each morning, I expect you to mind your manners,' I then told him. 'You must say, "Good morning, Your Highness. How do you fare?" '

" 'Ghooopmhakayuff?' The Thing That I Step On tried to mimic my words.

" 'That's for me to know and you to find out,' I replied haughtily. But soon he began to say the words almost like a normal boy. And on nights when I could not sleep, I would open my door and sit on him—now that his body was comfortably muscled—and I would tell him all my secrets: that I was afraid of lightning, that I had started growing armpit hair, and a hundred other things that I would never have told anyone else. The Thing That I Step On listened so nice and quietly, almost like a pet dog.

"And soon he began to learn the language through my chattering.

"The Royal Advisers had expected him to die in short order, but The Thing That I Step On was very obstinate, and he insisted upon living a little longer.

"One day I woke up in a gruesome mood and rang for

my Royal Spanker. She came immediately, carrying her black leather case, and tripped on The Thing That I Step On, breaking her front tooth in the process.

" 'Clumsy beast!' I shouted at her.

" 'Yeth, Your Highneth,' she said, lisping because of her broken tooth.

" 'I called you here to tell you that I intend to be very naughty today.'

" 'Yeth, Your Highneth.'

" 'So you are to fetch Klotchya, and tell her she is about to be spanked severely for my bad behavior.'

" 'But,' the Royal Spanker looked uncomfortable, 'Klotchya ith out with a headache.'

" 'Then fetch someone else! Quickly!' I was working myself up into a grand fury. 'My tantrum will begin in exactly sixty-three seconds!'

"The Royal Spanker curtsied and scuttered out to search for Klotchya's replacement, once again tripping on The Thing That I Step On.

" 'Sthupid, horrible boy–' she started to mutter, then smiled cruelly when she realized that she had found Klotchya's replacement. 'Oh, I will make you wail, my little friend,' she hissed at him as she pulled him to his feet. 'In payment for my tooth.'

"When the Royal Spanker brought The Thing That I Step On into my bedchamber, I was already pounding my fists against the wall and gnashing my teeth, and I admit I was caught off guard when I saw whom she had found to spank. For one thing, I didn't relish the thought of allowing The Thing That I Step On to watch me have a temper tantrum. And also, I wasn't sure I wanted to watch *him* getting spanked. It all seemed rather humiliating for the both of us.

"But, although it is very easy to start a temper tantrum, it is exceedingly difficult to stop one after it's been started. So I simply kept going, and after I had pulled out a hank of my own hair and kicked a hole in the wall and torn the curtains off all the windows, I collapsed onto my bed in utter exhaustion.

" 'Finished, Your Highneth?' the Royal Spanker asked.

" 'I believe so,' I said. Then I sat up and frowned. 'Wait . . .' I took off my shoe and hurled it at a painting on the wall. 'Okay, I'm finished.' I lay back on the bed, partly because I didn't want to see the expression on The Thing That I Step On's face after witnessing that.

" 'Exthellent,' the Royal Spanker said. She turned to The Thing That I Step On and smiled in a scary way. 'Remove your shirt, boy.'

"He did and I was surprised to see that he was strong and muscular and did not at all look like someone who would die in short order.

" 'The Printhepetha hath been very naughty and she muth be punished. But becauth she ith not allowed to cry, you mutht cry for her.' The Royal Spanker opened up her leather case. Inside were instruments of punishment tucked neatly in a red velvet lining: riding crops and wooden paddles and special hardwood sticks of varying sizes. With Klotchya, the Royal Spanker had always used the wooden paddle. Klotchya was such an excellent crier that it took only a few whacks of the paddle before she produced a very agreeable wail of pain. Truth be told, the Royal Spanker had wished that Klotchya was more of a challenge. She was a very gifted Spanker, and could produce a beautiful crescendo of pain if she had the right subject. She looked at the boy's strong back and smiled. Here, it seemed, was the challenge she'd been waiting for. She examined her instruments carefully and finally decided on a medium-sized stick. She picked it up and sliced it through the air a few times to hear its *shishhing* sound.

"I sat up in bed and held my breath. The Royal Spanker lifted her arm high, and brought the stick down hard on his back. The skin welted up right away–a mean red line of raised flesh—but The Thing That I Step On had not made a sound. He'd only shuddered the tiniest bit when the stick hit his back, but that was all.

"I frowned. That wasn't how Klotchya did it. Klotchya always sounded like she was being tortured to within an inch of her life, because that was her job.

"I got up then and stood before him. He looked down at me and I noticed for the first time that his eyes were intelligent-looking, and stubborn. I suppose I had never noticed before because I was usually stepping on him rather than looking at his face.

" 'I command you to cry,' I told him. Then I nodded to the Royal Spanker. 'Hit him again.'

"The Royal Spanker chose another stick. This one had tiny metal spikes along one end. The first time she struck him with it, his head reared back and his eyes shut, but he was silent.

" 'Why are you being so stubborn!?' I yelled at him, stamping my foot, feeling another tantrum coming on. 'All I'm requiring is that you cry. I have been naughty and *someone* must cry, and it cannot be me. You must do it for me. It's as simple as that. You can fake it, even, I don't care. Hit him again.'

"The Royal Spanker hit him again and again, until his

back was crosshatched with red welts tipped with blood and he was covered with sweat, and still he would not cry. I felt my face grow hot with anger and shame. Never in my life had someone refused to do what I asked.

" 'Why? Why won't you?! You are the most horrible boy I have ever met! I'm sorry we brought you here in the first place. I wish you were back in your stupid cave with your stupid hairy cave family . . .' I screamed on and on, so loudly that the other Royal Servants came running. They stood outside the door, staring at me with their eyes wide and frightened. Finally I stopped screaming and glowered up at him, waiting for an explanation.

"The Thing That I Step On looked at me, his eyes woozy with pain, but still stubborn and completely dry. 'Why should I cry,' he replied, 'when you have been crying for the both of us since the first stroke hit my back?'

"I touched my face and felt that it was wet. I *had* been crying. I had shed my precious tears, all of them. They were already evaporating on my cheek.

"The other servants rushed over now, and tried to wring out the part of my dress on which my tears had fallen, hoping to salvage whatever they could. But it was hopeless. There was not a drop to be had.

" 'Why didn't you tell me I was crying?!' I screeched at

the Royal Spanker. She had certainly seen that I was crying, but because she didn't want that to spoil her own fun, she hadn't told me.

"I collapsed then, and I was put into bed. I fell violently ill from the shock and grief, and for many days I was delirious with fever. When I finally awoke, the first thing I thought was: I am in love with The Thing That I Step On. I love him so deeply that my feet are now aching to walk on him once more. I have lost all my priceless tears out of pity for The Thing That I Step On, which means that no prince will ever marry me, but I don't care, because The Thing That I Step On is worth a hundred lousy princes to me.

"I stretched out my body, which felt oddly stiff, and I put on my slippers and ran to open my bedchamber door so that I could tell him that I loved him and that we should run away together and live in a cave . . . well, perhaps not a *cave,* maybe just a modest three-bedroom ranch house. But as I lifted my right leg, so as to step on The Thing That I Step On, I found he wasn't there.

"I screamed until the servants came running. I demanded that they fetch The Thing That I Step On. They looked down at the floor and then at each other.

" 'Have you all gone deaf?' I cried. 'I said fetch him!'

" 'He is gone, Your Highness,' one of the servants said nervously.

" 'Gone?! Well, find him and bring him back!'

" 'He has run away, Your Highness. Rumor has it that he sailed with a fishing vessel headed for Japan. And wisely so, since, if you recall, the punishment for making the Princepessa cry is death.'

"I was heartbroken. Since I had used up all my tears, I could not cry, so the sorrow worked its way inward and settled in a little hard clot of sadness, right here." The Princepessa Christina Lilli touched her belly. "So, you see, I have never been 'almost kissed' like your Romeo and Juliet. I have never been kissed at all. The only reminder I have of him is draped across the back of your chair."

Olivia turned to see what that was. The fur wrap.

"It was made of his bearskin, which he had left on the floor outside my door. I've kept it all this time. Silly of me." The Princepessa shrugged.

"I'm sorry, Christina Lilli. But maybe he'll show up here one day," Olivia said. "You never know." But she doubted it, and from the Princepessa's halfhearted "Perhaps" it seemed that the Princepessa doubted it also.

"You know, child," the Princepessa said, "you do look

so lovely in that wrap, and I think it's time I let it go. I will give it to you as a gift."

"No–" Olivia tried to protest, but the Princepessa would hear none of it. The waiter returned with desserts. They didn't come on a cart, like Olivia had hoped, but there were the most delicious little cakes and pastries, and Olivia found that she had just enough room in her belly to try one of each.

The first thing Olivia did when she came back to the brownstone was whip off the wrap. It was itchy and hot, and it didn't smell too great either. She opened the hallway closet and hung it up there, since she didn't really want it smelling up her own bedroom. Then she opened the double doors to the lagoon.

The room was entirely dark. There was no sound, except for the soft lapping of water against the edge of the marble. In a moment Olivia noticed a small circular yellow light floating in the blackness, just above the water. It moved slowly across the length of the lagoon, and only when Olivia's eyes had adjusted to the dark could she see that it was the light on the front of a boat that was drifting aimlessly in the water. Olivia could detect the outline of a person in the boat, and she tentatively said, "Hello?"

There was a moment's pause and then: "Is that you, Olivia?" The voice belonged unmistakably to Ansel, although it sounded oddly flat, almost scared.

"Yes," Olivia said, her voice cool and distrustful.

"Oh, I am so relieved!" Ansel cried. "I was beginning to worry that our little household was falling apart completely. But you're back, thank heavens! Now we must simply hope and pray for his speedy recovery. Then we'll all be quite happy again, won't we?"

"Hope for whose speedy recovery?" Olivia asked.

"Your father, of course! Poor, dear George! Oh. But you haven't heard. No, of course you haven't."

Olivia felt a rush of fear snaking through her chest.

"What happened to him?" Olivia asked faintly.

"Well, we don't really know. He simply collapsed in his room. We heard a terrific thump upstairs, and when Nora went to look, she found him on the floor, unconscious."

Olivia let out a panicked cry. She ran to one of the boats and began to frantically untie the rope from its mooring, but Ansel hastened to add, "No, he's not here, my dear. We've had him taken to the hospital. Don't worry, he's getting the best possible care. I have seen to that personally. They're running tests, many tests, and they will have this all sussed out in no time, my dear, and then we will have our delightful George returned to us as good as new . . . as good as new." His voice broke and it seemed to Olivia that he might be close to tears. She hated him for that. Her body was shaking and she wanted to scream at him and demand to know what he had done to her father. For she was certain that he *had* done something to make her father sick, maybe the same thing that he had done to the redheaded man. And the redheaded man had died! She struggled to control herself, took a deep breath.

"Which hospital?" she asked icily.

"St. Sebastian's, my dear, on Sixty-eighth Street. But you'll have to wait until tomorrow to see him. They've sent all visitors away for the evening." Ansel rowed over to her and held out his hand to help her aboard. "Come," he said. "You might as well go upstairs and get some rest."

"I can row myself, thank you," Olivia snapped. She finished untying the boat, jumped in, and pushed off the ledge with a quick shove of her hand. Upstairs, she went into her father's room first. There was nothing amiss except that one of the blankets from his bed was in a heap on the floor, as though he had grabbed on to it before he collapsed.

She went into her own room, shut the door, and locked it quickly. Then she got into bed without even taking off her dress and curled up in a ball. All sorts of horrible thoughts passed through her mind: Suppose her father died–how could she bear it?! And what would happen to her then? Would she have to go to California and live with her mother? She didn't think her mother would be too happy about that, and neither would Olivia. She began to sob heavily, and she kept sobbing until she couldn't anymore, and was simply sucking in her breath in large gusty gasps.

"Christopher. Christopher!" she called to him silently. She waited, and in a moment she heard a voice in the far distance. It was Christopher, she was sure of it, but his words were muffled. His voice came and went, and finally drifted away altogether. She remembered that he'd told her it was hard for him to reach her when she was very upset. She tried to calm herself, but a fresh wave of tears came instead, and she cried and cried until finally, exhausted, she dropped off to sleep.

NINE

The morning arrived, gray and clammy. There was a heavy feeling in the air, as if the whole city were saturated with moisture. For a moment Olivia struggled to recall all the events of yesterday—they seemed to merge into each other, forming a confusing tapestry. Olivia picked it apart, separating the threads until she remembered all the bits and pieces. Foremost in her memory was the fact that her father was ill, and that Ansel had said she could visit him in the hospital today.

She hastily changed her clothes and escaped from the house as quickly and quietly as possible, managing to avoid seeing Ansel and Nora. She knew exactly where St. Sebastian's Hospital was. A few years back, when she had broken her arm, her father had taken her to their emergency room.

As she walked, rain sputtered then stopped, but a few blocks before the hospital it returned again, this time in a heavy downpour. Olivia ran the rest of the way, and by the time she reached the hospital, she looked like she had jumped into a swimming pool with all her clothes on.

At the front desk she told them she was there to see George Kidney. Her insides trembled a little as she said his name–she was afraid the receptionist would shake her head sadly and tell her that George Kidney was a very sick man . . . or worse . . . but the woman only plunked her fingernails on the computer keyboard and looked at the screen.

"Third floor," the woman said blandly. She scribbled *Third Floor* on an orange sticker marked VISITOR and handed it to Olivia. "Put this on and check in at the nurses' station. Elevator's to your right."

"Thanks," Olivia said, feeling relieved somehow that the woman had sounded like she was bored with her job.

The elevator was the type that felt like it wasn't moving at all, and just when Olivia was convinced that it was stuck between floors, the doors slid open on the third floor. She quickly stepped out into a purple waiting room with a long desk on one side, behind which was a chubby nurse in round glasses, wearing lipstick that matched the color of the walls.

"Yes?" she said flatly without looking at Olivia.

"Hello," Olivia said. "I'm here to visit George Kidney. I'm his daughter."

"Oh." The nurse looked up at Olivia and smiled with her purple lips. "Nice fellow, that Mr. Kidney."

"How is he?" Olivia asked, her stomach tightening with dread.

"Well, he's had a rough night of it. Go on in and see him. He's in Room Twenty-six. His last visitor just left."

Olivia walked down the hall, smelling the bitter lemony smell of disinfectant and catching the quiet, solemn scraps of conversation as she passed by patients' rooms. It was an all-too-familiar sensation. When Christopher was sick with cancer, she visited him every day. It was a different hospital, but the smell and the sounds were the same. The thought that Christopher had actually died in that hospital made her walk faster now, so fast that she walked right past Room 26, and had to backtrack.

The door was open and the room was festooned with flowers–in a tall vase on the night table, in a short vase on the television set, in vases on the floor and on the windowsill. There were even bouquets of flowers wrapped in cones and lying on the bed. In fact, there were so many flowers that Olivia did not see her father at first.

"Dad?" she asked hesitantly.

"Sweetpea!" George's face emerged from behind a huge paper cone full of roses that was resting on his pillow. He was wan and pale, his eyes were puffy, and his body looked sort of sad and spindly in his hospital gown. Olivia walked up to him, careful to navigate between the vases on the floor, while George collected the cones of flowers on his bed and put them down by his feet so that Olivia could sit beside him.

Olivia now could see that he had a tube in his arm that was attached to a plastic bag on a pole by his bed–just like Christopher had.

"That's no big deal, Sweetpea, really," he told her when he saw her staring at it, and he reached out and squeezed her hand reassuringly, knowing what she was thinking.

"Oh, Dad . . . what happened?" Olivia asked, trying to hold back tears.

"Well, according to the doctors, I was poisoned," he said. Olivia bit her lip to keep from crying out. So she was right. Ansel *had* done this to him.

"How?" Olivia whispered.

"In the most atrocious, dreadful way you can imagine," he whispered back, his eyes glancing at the hallway to make sure no one else was listening. Olivia swallowed thickly and leaned in toward him.

"I was poisoned by dessert," George said.

"Dessert?!"

George nodded. "It was Nora's pie that did me in. It just *looked* so good, and I thought, Well, what can she possibly do to mess up pie? But according to the doctors, the berries she put in it must have been poisonous. I was pretty sick for a while, but it looks like I'll be just fine, no permanent damage. They want me to stay another night and, knock on wood, they'll be sending me home tomorrow afternoon."

"Oh, Dad!" Olivia felt a tremendous surge of relief. She wouldn't lose her father. She wouldn't have to worry about where she would live, or who would want her. She threw herself on him roughly to hug him, and then quickly pulled back. "Sorry, did I hurt you? Sorry, sorry, but I'm so happy it was just the pie!"

But then she remembered the red-haired man.

"What's wrong?" George asked her, noting that her expression had changed abruptly.

"Nothing. I was thinking about Ansel," Olivia said cautiously.

"You just missed him!" George's face lighted up. "He was the one who brought all the flowers. The man's a little eccentric, but he's definitely the nicest boss I've ever had. And you should see him salsa dance!"

Olivia opened her mouth to tell him about the red-headed man, but stopped herself. She just didn't have the heart to make her father worry—not now, while he was still in the hospital.

She sat with him a while longer and amused him with the story of the underground Babatavian restaurant and how the Babatavians put wigs on their babies (which George thought was so funny that he made Olivia repeat it three times).

"I'll be back tomorrow, Dad," Olivia promised at the end of her visit, and she gave her father another hug, more carefully this time.

She headed for the elevator, but then thought better of it. There had to be stairs someplace. Coming up the hall was a brisk young woman in a striped uniform, one of the hospital volunteers, wheeling a clattering cart full of newspapers and magazines and paperback books and candy.

"Excuse me," Olivia said. "Are there stairs anywhere?"

"Sure. You go left up that hallway, then make a right where the hallway splits, and—oh, I'll just show you, it's easier."

The young woman turned her cart around and started back the way she'd come, with Olivia following her. As they moved through the hallway, the woman stuck her head into patients' rooms and greeted them merrily.

"Hi, Mrs. Gribitz, how's the swelling?" Then, after they passed Mrs. Gribitz's room, she turned to Olivia and said, "Nice lady. Loves the cheesy supermarket tabloid papers—you know, the ones where they show women who give birth to three-headed pig-babies or German shepherds who can speak German. She believes it all too! Oh, hi there, Mr. Farkus! How's the nose?" Then quietly to Olivia, "He stuck a saltshaker up his nose, just to see if it would fit, and it got stuck. You couldn't *pay* me to eat at his house!" She chatted on and on until they reached a pair of glass doors marked EAST WING.

"Almost there," she said as they passed through the doors.

The East Wing was very different from the part of the hospital Olivia's father was in. Here, it was very quiet. There were not as many visitors walking about, and even the chatty young volunteer grew quiet as they walked through the halls. She greeted very few patients, and when she did, she spoke very softly and without the cheery commentary to Olivia. As they passed one room, Olivia glimpsed a pair of terribly thin legs sticking out of a hospital gown. A screen blocked the upper part of the patient's body from Olivia's view.

"It's her birthday in two days," the volunteer said when

she noticed Olivia staring. "She'll be twenty-two years old. The nurses are going to do up her hair nicely and we'll have a little party for her. Her family probably won't even come." She shook her head and clucked her tongue. "They stopped visiting a few months ago. I suppose some people would wonder why we're bothering to celebrate her birthday at all. They'd say that she doesn't even know we're celebrating it. But, personally, I think she *does* know. Deep down."

"What's wrong with her?" Olivia asked.

"She's in a coma. Has been for months. I said they ought to put her in one of the rooms that face Central Park—you know, let her listen to all the kids clamoring in the playground and the dogs barking. Just so's to keep her mind occupied."

The mention of Central Park made Olivia think of something. St. Sebastian's was probably the hospital nearest to the band shell. She glanced at the volunteer—the woman was so chatty, and she seemed to know all the patients. It was worth a try.

"When I was in Central Park yesterday," Olivia said, "an ambulance took away a man who was lying on a bench in the band shell pavilion. I think he was dead."

"Yesterday? Oooh, yes, yes, I heard the nurses talking about him. Poor soul. Bad ticker," she said, tapping her chest. "Had a heart attack while he was sitting in the park, reading. They tried to resuscitate him, but," she shook her head, "he was as dead as a doornail. And voila–" The cart lady pointed to the sign for the stairs. "Here you go!" Olivia thanked her and the woman careened her cart around and headed back down the hall.

A heart attack. Then it had nothing to do with Ansel after all. Olivia felt relieved, but also embarrassed at having suspected him. She was extremely glad that she hadn't said anything about it to Nora or her father.

Outside, the rain had stopped and the sun was coming out again, even as rumbles of thunder were dying away in the distance. The streets were still glistening from the rain, and the cars were making wonderful *shlushing* sounds against the pavement, like mayonnaise being pressed into egg salad–a sound Olivia loved. When she thought her father might be dying, the world had seemed like a cramped dark box in which she wanted to curl up and hide. Now the day stretched out before her, dazzlingly brilliant, and she recalled that she hadn't practiced on Jezebel since seeing the red-haired man in the park.

She ran hard all the way back to the brownstone, enjoying the feel of the breeze against her face, and of her hair as it bounced against the back of her neck. She darted around people on the streets, suddenly imagining that she was riding on Jezebel and that Christopher was with her. She was flying at top speed, in perfect balance, jumping over curbs, somersaulting in the air and landing squarely on Jezebel again, while Christopher was laughing in breathless amazement at her skill! Olivia ran between a man and a woman, who stepped aside quickly to let her through, and she thought jubilantly, That's right, people! Get out of my way! Olivia Kidney stops for no one!

TEN

Olivia reached the brownstone in no time. She changed out of her wet clothes, grabbed Jezebel, and ran back outside again.

The street was quiet as usual, and she didn't feel like running into Ruben in the park, so she put the skateboard down and practiced up and down the sidewalk. It was a little bumpy, and there was a large slab of broken pavement jutting up, which she took care to avoid. After a few runs, she found that when she bent her legs a little, she could keep her balance better. She still stuck her arms out to the sides like a tightrope walker, but as long as no one was watching, she didn't care.

She suddenly thought about when Ruben had ridden Jezebel, and she felt a rush of jealousy. He had looked so easy and natural on her, the way Christopher looked when he rode her. In a burst of determination, Olivia bent her legs a little deeper, then jumped, just like Ruben had done. The board didn't jump with her and she landed on the edge of it, so that it flipped up and smashed painfully against the side of her thigh.

"Naughty board," she heard someone say. She turned around and saw Nora peeking out from behind the front door. Nora stuck her arm through the door's opening and waved a sandwich in the air. "Thought you might be hungry." When Olivia hesitated, she added, "Don't worry. It's just peanut butter and jelly. No mystery ingredients."

Olivia *was* pretty hungry. She picked up her board, walked up the stairs, and took the sandwich.

"You're not too good on that thing, are you, kid?" Nora said, still hovering behind the partially open door.

"I'll get better," Olivia said confidently, and she took a bite out of the sandwich.

"Hey, sorry about your dad. I mean, I feel pretty guilty. Ansel was furious with me."

"Well, I guess you didn't *mean* to poison him," Olivia said.

"That's what I told Ansel!" Nora agreed. "But he doesn't see it that way. He says that he wouldn't be surprised if your dad packed up his things and left."

"Nah, he wouldn't," Olivia reassured her, chewing away.

"He says Ansel is the best boss he's ever had. I don't think he'd leave unless Ansel fired him."

"Fired him?" Nora said, clearly perplexed. "Fired him from what?"

"From the handyman's job," Olivia said.

"What handyman's job?" Nora asked.

"Ansel hired him to be a live-in handyman." Olivia shot Nora a puzzled look. How could Nora not know that?

"No, he didn't," Nora said.

"Of course he did," Olivia said, beginning to lose her patience. "That's why we're here. We got the note under our door, and the money . . ."

"Not from Ansel, kid."

"But, then . . . why did he take us in?"

"Why?" Nora shrugged. "Because you two seemed to want to stay."

"Then who put the note under our door? Who gave us the first two weeks' payment?"

"Beats me."

How odd! No wonder Ansel hadn't given her father anything to do around the house. But why on earth would he just take strangers in off the street? Well, maybe Ansel wasn't *bad and dangerous,* as Ms. Bender had declared, but it certainly seemed like he might be *mad.*

"Anyway," Nora continued, "Ansel has absolutely forbidden me to cook anything ever again. His mother's coming tonight, and I was going to make this great big dinner, but he says he's not taking any more chances. I mean, come on, it's not like I'm going to use any more *berries* in my cooking."

"To be honest, Nora, you're not too good a cook, even when you don't poison people," Olivia said.

Nora looked a little hurt, then retorted, "Yeah? Well, I can cook better than you can do an ollie."

"A what?"

"An ollie. That thing you were *trying* to do when your board attacked you."

"Do you skateboard?" Olivia asked.

"Used to. Back in the day."

"Will you show me how to do an ollie?" Olivia asked.

"Now?"

Olivia held the skateboard up to the partly open door. "Please."

Nora looked at the board as though she were afraid to touch it. She ran a hand through her hair, then after a moment, opened the door wider and grabbed Jezebel. She smiled a little as she held the board, flicking the wheels with her fingers to make them spin. Then she stepped outside and ran down the stairs quickly, as if she were afraid someone would stop her.

She put down the board and took off her shoes. Then she got on the board and pushed off. Her first run up the street was a little tentative, as though she were getting used to the feel of Jezebel beneath her bare feet. On the way back, however, she picked up speed. She deliberately rode over the large slab of broken pavement so that the board jumped up a little and clattered back down. Then she sped up even more, flying past Olivia, heading straight for a fire hydrant. Olivia screamed, "Watch out!" but Nora popped Jezebel up with a wild but agile leap. Both Nora and Jezebel jumped right over the hydrant, and Nora was off again, faster and faster.

Olivia remembered that Nora had said staying in the house kept her out of trouble. Now Olivia could see why. Nora was laughing out loud, her short black hair flying wildly in all directions as she swiveled around abruptly and headed straight for the stairs of one of the other brownstones. She popped Jezebel up so that they leapt over six steps and then made Jezebel leap once more to the stairs' stone banister, which they slid back down, then slammed onto the pavement and sped away. Olivia was so amazed, she stood up to cheer and clap as Nora flew past her.

Marching toward them from the far end of the street was what looked like an army regiment wearing black helmets, black leather boots, and crisp tan-and-white uniforms, and all carrying black sticks. They walked double file, led by a blond woman who was barking orders at them the whole way. It took Olivia a moment to realize that the woman was Ms. Bender and the marching troop was the students at Ms. Bender's School for Superior Children, dressed in horseback-riding gear.

"Beirut, if you persist in not keeping your heels down in the stirrups, I'll attach weights to your boots! Dijon . . . as usual you were hopeless. You jiggled around on that horse like a human bean bag! How do you expect—"

All of a sudden the troop of children scattered as Nora flew toward them, yipping and whooping. Ms. Bender didn't move as quickly as her students, however, and when she saw Nora, she panicked and sidestepped, tripping on the broken piece of pavement and falling onto her hands and knees.

Aiming directly for Ms. Bender, Nora called back to Olivia, "Okay, kid, watch closely! Here comes your ollie!" A split second before she reached the horrified Ms. Bender, Nora smacked the tail end of the board to the pavement with her back foot and slid her front foot forward to the board's nose. Jezebel popped up, and both Nora and Jezebel leapt over Ms. Bender and landed solidly on the other side of her.

"Holy cow, she is really insane!" Olivia cried out loud.

Some of Ms. Bender's students, including Frannie, clapped and whistled. Ms. Bender slapped furiously at their legs with her riding crop as she struggled to her feet.

"Riffraff!" she screamed after Nora. "Street rat!"

Nora had reached the corner, and now she pivoted sharply and raced back up the street toward Ms. Bender, who plastered herself against the side of a building in terror while the students rushed to either side of the street to let Nora through.

Suddenly, Nora stopped. Her face crumpled in pain, and she stumbled off the board and bent over double. Her arms wrapped around her middle and Olivia could hear her gasping for air and whimpering.

"Nora!" Olivia cried, running down the steps to help her, but Nora waved her off and began to stagger back to the brownstone. Her face was glassy with perspiration and alarmingly pale. She grabbed the banister—nearly flung herself upon it—and made her way up the brownstone stairs, taking slow, agonizing steps.

By now Ms. Bender had collected herself. She gathered up her students and pointed a manicured finger at Nora. "*That,* children," she said, her voice full of powerful indignation, "is what we call trash. And although trash can be irritating, in the end that woman's life will make no impression upon the world whatsoever."

Olivia glared at Ms. Bender before retrieving Jezebel and following Nora back inside the house. Nora collapsed in a chair by the hallway desk, a little slumped over, but already Olivia could hear that her breathing was growing more regular.

"Nora, are you okay?" Olivia asked softly.

"Sure, sure. I'll be fine. I don't know what I was thinking, going outside like that, what with my agoraphobia and all." Nora shook her head. She was still pale but her face had lost that horrifying expression of pain. "Anyway," she said, smiling a little shakily at Olivia, "that's how you do an ollie, kid."

Eleven

"Olivia!"

Olivia's eyes snapped open as she lay in bed that night. It was still dark outside, but she was sure she had heard her name being called.

"Olivia! Hey!" The voice was calling to her from outside—not from the window that faced the street but from the one that faced Ms. Bender's School for Superior Children.

Olivia opened the window and leaned out, staring into the night.

"Well, hallelujah, praise the Lord. It's Lazarus raised from the dead! I've been calling your name for practically ten minutes," said a semi-whispered voice. Olivia saw Frannie, only a few feet away, leaning out—dangerously far, Olivia thought—of a very tiny window in Ms. Bender's school. The window was so small—probably just a bathroom window—that only someone Frannie's size could have fit through it.

"What do you want?" Olivia said grumpily.

"A good deed. I need you to get my sister out of your house."

"How do you know she's here?"

"I had a feeling she was going to try something tonight. She's been acting funny for the past couple of weeks—kind of out of it, you know. Gazing off at nothing, hardly eating. And then Ms. Bender caught her writing Ansel's name in her notebook during French class, with little hearts all around it. I think she's got a crazy mad crush on him. Today she seemed a little happier than usual and she actually ate most of her dinner, so I had a feeling something was up. She sleeps down the hall from me, so I didn't see when she left, but I've been keeping an eye on your front door all night, and I saw her go up your stairs. Look, if Ms. Bender catches her, she'll make Dijon's life miserable—even *more* miserable, I should say."

"What do you want *me* to do about it?" Olivia asked.

"Just find her and tell her that if she doesn't get back here this minute, I'm going to call Mom tomorrow and tell her what she's been doing."

Olivia groaned. "Okay, fine." Olivia pulled her head

back, then leaned out again. "And by the way, who's Lazarus?" she asked.

"Oh, for goodness' sake, Olivia, get thee to a library." Frannie shook her head, then disappeared back inside the school.

She's sort of dorky, Olivia thought, but not bad, really.

Olivia put on her bathrobe and started down the stairs as quietly as she could. She had not quite reached the second floor when she heard voices below. She backed up on the stairs, crouched down, and waited.

In a moment she heard a girl's voice saying, "I've wanted to come here for a real long time. It's all I ever think about."

I bet that's Dijon, Olivia thought.

"Are you quite sure, my dear? You seem very young. Perhaps you are making a mistake . . ." This was Ansel's voice.

"I'm *absolutely* sure," she said stoutly.

"Well, we can talk about it a little more later. In the meantime, you must meet the others," Ansel said. "We have a rather interesting crowd tonight." And then there was the sound of keys jangling and a lock turning. Olivia peeked around and saw the second-floor door open. She readied herself, and as soon as Ansel and Dijon went in, Olivia jumped down, flying over four steps to the second-story landing, and grabbed the edge of the door before it slammed shut. She waited a second, but when she heard nothing, she slipped through the door.

In front of her was a narrow, curving hallway with a red carpet. There were doors on both sides of the hall, all of them numbered and shut. Cautiously, Olivia walked down the hallway, listening for voices. She had followed the first curve of the hallway, then the second, when she began to hear a strange cacophony of sounds—a cooing and then horrible shrieking that rose in pitch by degrees until it suddenly stopped. Then the cooing started up again. The noises seemed to be coming from a door on her left, marked 23. Olivia pressed her ear to the door and indeed could hear the cooing coming from within the room.

"If you're here to pick one out, you'd better do it now," a voice said behind her. Olivia turned and saw a large man with a rough but forlorn-looking face, wearing white coveralls. "I bet you anything all the good ones are already taken. That would be just my luck. I got the worst luck youse ever heard of."

The man opened the door, which caused a terrific ruckus inside the room—screeching and thumping and howling. Inside was what looked to be a chaotic pet shop. There were sleek black crows perched on bare-leafed trees stuck in large pots, cawing stridently. There were downy white owls screeching in cages, several glass jars with large pearl-winged moths darting around inside, and a single white pigeon that kept flying into one of the windows, cracking its head against the glass, dropping to the ground, then getting up and flying into the window again.

"See! What did I tell youse!" the man cried in dismay. "They've all been taken!"

"What do you mean?" Olivia asked.

The man pointed to the red tags that were tied to the legs of all the crows. Olivia looked around and saw that indeed all the owls had red tags attached to their legs too, and even the moths had red tags tied to the neck of their jars. Olivia had no idea what this meant, but she didn't want to waste time finding out.

"Excuse me," Olivia said to the man, who was now walking around the room, shaking his head each time he found a red tag, "but have you seen a girl with shoulder-length frizzy reddish hair, about sixteen years old?"

"What?" he said. "A girl with reddish hair . . . yeah, I seen someone like that—Oh! Wouldn't ya know it! Ain't that just my luck!" He was watching the white pigeon that was slamming into the window. "The only one left is the pigeon! An ordinary pigeon! Well, that's just humiliating, if you ask me. Don't my bad luck beat all?" The pigeon had gotten to its feet again, flapped its wings clumsily, and flew off, only to ram back into the window. Olivia winced at the sound of its head against the pane.

"So . . . the girl with reddish hair . . . where did you see her?"

The man had taken a red tag out of his back pocket and was squatting on the floor, trying to grab hold of the pigeon before it took off again.

"Where? Let me think . . . yeah, I seen her standing outside Room Fifty-eight—ooof!" The bird had squirmed out of his hands and was heading directly for the window again.

"Thanks," Olivia said, and she started to leave.

"But she won't be there anymore," the man added. "She'll be with the rest of 'em in the Stygian Theater."

"A theater?" Olivia rolled her eyes. It looked like she was going to spend the rest of the night chasing down Frannie's sister. "What street is that on?"

"Street? What are you talking, street?" The man had finally managed to capture the pigeon and was tying his tag to its leg. "It's just at the end of this hallway."

Relieved, but confused, Olivia closed the door and started down the hallway. It curved this way and that, and at some point appeared to be spiraling in on itself. Finally, on her right, she saw a sign that said STYGIAN THEATER in pink lights that flashed on and off. Below the sign was a heavy wooden door, which Olivia pulled open.

"Program?" asked an elderly woman who was standing just inside with an armful of theater programs and holding a flashlight. She wore a little plastic pin that said USHER. She smiled at Olivia and handed her a little booklet. On its cover was printed in gold letters, *Into the Woods . . . For Good.*

"I'd suggest sitting a little to the right–that's where most of the action takes place." The usher winked at Olivia.

It was a small theater, and most of the twenty or so people in there were sitting up front. Olivia spotted Dijon sitting among them, and she walked down the aisle until she came to Dijon's row.

"Dijon," Olivia said. She tried to say it quietly, but Dijon was chatting away with the person seated next to her, so Olivia had to raise her voice. "Hey, Dijon."

Dijon turned and looked at Olivia blankly.

"I'm a friend of your sister's," Olivia told her. "She says you need to get back to the school before Ms. Bender finds out you're missing."

Dijon's face turned pink and she replied heatedly, "Tell her to mind her own business."

The lights suddenly dimmed, and on stage a row of footlights lighted up.

"Come on, Dijon," Olivia persisted. "She said if you don't, she'll tell your moth–"

"I'm sorry, young lady"–the usher came up to Olivia, shining a flashlight–"but you'll have to take your seat now. The play is about to begin."

"But I just want to–" Olivia started to object.

"Shh!" the usher said, and she firmly guided Olivia toward a seat on the right side of the theater. Just as Olivia sat down, the man in the coveralls rushed into the theater, which earned him a reproachful look from the usher. She hurriedly gave him a program and sat him directly behind Olivia.

"What'd I miss?" he leaned forward and asked her breathlessly.

"Nothing. It's just starting," Olivia whispered back.

"Oh, good! I hear this one's a doozy! Real blood-and-guts kind of stuff."

Up on stage the curtain was rising slowly, revealing a woodland scene. The stage was covered with cardboard pine trees and bushes and ferns, and all around was the sound of birds chirping and cicadas chittering. In a minute a woman dressed in khaki hiking shorts and a matching khaki shirt with pink hiking boots walked on stage. She was accompanied by a black-haired man wearing tortoise-shell glasses.

"Isn't it perfectly delicious, Frank?" the woman said in a breathless, excited voice. "I know we were supposed to go to Puerto Vallarta for our honeymoon, but now I'm glad we didn't. Don't you love being in the woods? Do you know what we should do, Frank? We should build a delicious little house in the middle of the woods, darling."

"Well, I'm not sure if that's such a good idea, Lillian. You know how I feel about bugs," the man said, swatting at flies.

Behind Olivia, the man in the coveralls snorted. "Loser," he muttered.

"And then we'll have three perfectly delicious little children, and we won't ever allow them to watch television, so as not to spoil their delicious little minds—"

"Lillian, did you hear something?" the man asked, nervously looking around the cardboard woods. It was then that Olivia realized that the man on stage was Ansel. What with his glasses, a black wig, and a sad little droop in his shoulders, he was nearly unrecognizable.

"And perhaps you'll grow one of those delicious beards that woodsmen grow—a tidy one, of course, nothing too scratchy . . ."

Suddenly a bear emerged from behind one of the pine trees. It wasn't a real bear, Olivia was almost certain, but a person in a bear suit. Still, the suit was very realistic-looking, and the person playing the bear walked on all fours in a slow, very bearlike swagger.

"Heads up, lady!" This came from the man in the coveralls, and the usher pointed her flashlight on him and whispered, "Control yourself."

Ansel's character said in a low voice, "Lillian, *do not move a muscle.*"

". . . but you'll have to be careful when you're eating corn, of course," Lillian continued, without noticing the bear behind her. "There's nothing more disgusting than corn niblets in a man's beard–"

"Lillian!" Ansel's character cut her off sharply. "There is a bear standing right behind you." The bear had risen up on its hind legs and was growling.

Lillian turned around, looked at the bear, and in a very small voice said, "Oh, crap."

Olivia bit her lip nervously. She knew it was just a play, but there was something genuinely frightening about it nevertheless.

Lillian looked at the bear and the bear looked at Lillian. Then the bear dropped down to all fours again, threw its head back, and sounded a ghastly roar before charging directly at her. Lillian screamed and the bear pounced on her, emitting fearsome snarls and bellows, and then the stage went dark and silent. The curtain fell.

"I bet she tasted perfectly delicious," the man in the coveralls whispered. Olivia smiled, but she didn't laugh. In fact, she suddenly felt rather heavyhearted.

The stage lights came on again and the curtain rose. Ansel walked on stage to take a bow, and the audience clapped like mad. Then the bear came out and someone hissed, but Ansel shook his head and more clapping began. The bear took his bear head off, and inside was a middle-aged woman with glasses. Finally, Lillian came running on stage, laughing, and the audience rose to give her a standing ovation, even the man in coveralls.

The clapping went on and on, until finally the actors, holding hands, ran off stage. The lights in the theater were turned up, and people were rising to leave. It was then that Olivia noticed that Dijon was gone–she had probably slipped out during the play.

Olivia shook her head, irritated. "Well, I'm not going to chase Dijon all night long. If she wants to be an idiot, that's her decision."

Olivia stood up to leave, and the man in the coveralls

held out his hand. He looked at her very strangely–in other words he really, really looked at her, which most people don't do.

"Good luck," he said very earnestly.

"Okay," Olivia said, not exactly sure what he was referring to. "Same to you."

He shrugged and replied, "Good luck ain't never been my strong point. But thanks anyways."

TWELVE

The following day, as Olivia headed over to St. Sebastian's, she wondered about what she had seen the night before. Was Ansel running some kind of a weird theater group? There were lots of groups like that in New York–Olivia knew because her mother had belonged to one of them where everyone wore white bodysuits and black socks and gloves, and jumped around on stage while someone read poetry. At least the play last night had had a story . . . sort of. But what about the room full of birds? Maybe Ansel used them in his plays somehow.

At St. Sebastian's Olivia took the hospital stairs up the three flights into the East Wing, where she passed by the room of the girl in a coma. The girl's door was closed this time. In a way Olivia was glad. She didn't want to see those sad, thin legs again, yet she knew that if the door had been open, she would have looked.

She wound through the hallways, getting lost once or twice, until she reached the West Wing. When she approached her father's room, she found that he already had company. Sitting on a chair beside his bed was an elderly woman in a hospital gown, with long silver hair tied back in a thick, lumpy braid. She was reading to George from a tabloid newspaper:

". . . and when she opened up the package of frozen fish sticks, she found six alien babies inside, frozen solid!" She looked up from her reading, waiting for George's reaction.

"Were they in a batter?" George asked.

"A batter?" the woman asked.

"You know," George said, "a fish-stick batter?"

"Oooh." The woman's eyes widened. "Well, I don't know. Let me see . . ." She looked back down at the article.

"Hi, Dad," Olivia said as she walked into the room.

"Oh, hi, Sweetpea!" He looked a lot better today. The color had returned to his face and he'd sort of combed his hair. "This is Mrs. Gribitz. She's been reading to me from her newspapers all afternoon."

"Nope." Mrs. Gribitz looked up from her paper and shook her head. "Doesn't appear to have been any batter involved. It says here that the woman let the aliens defrost for twenty minutes. Then they all stood up and asked her where the nearest ATM was. When she told them, they disappeared down the drain in the kitchen sink."

Olivia rolled her eyes at her father, but George politely responded, "Amazing!"

"Isn't it?" Mrs. Gribitz said. "The world is chock-full of amazing things." She turned the pages of her paper and said, "Listen to this one . . ." and she began to read an article about a girl on the Chinese Olympic swim team who had been thrown out of the competition because it had been discovered that she was actually a mermaid.

Olivia guessed this was going to go on for a while, so she sat down on the bed next to her father. As Mrs. Gribitz read to them about the Chinese mermaid, Olivia gazed out the window. It wasn't much of a view–just the old redbrick building next door. She looked into the window of the facing apartment, whose shade was drawn. Olivia could make out shadowy forms moving around inside. She wondered if that was how the girl in the coma saw things–all dim and faded, as though everything were behind window shades. Or maybe she saw nothing at all and just dreamed all the time. Olivia tried to imagine what that would be like, and decided she wouldn't like it, since some of those dreams were bound to be nightmares, and if you didn't ever wake up, you'd think the nightmares were real.

". . . isn't that just the oddest story?" Mrs. Gribitz asked after she had finished the article. "You would have thought her coaches would have noticed that she grew a tail in the water! Do you know," she said sadly, "sometimes I wonder if these stories are really true."

"I don't know, Mrs. Gribitz, strange things *do* happen," said George, who hated to see people disappointed. "Why, just on the Channel Five news this afternoon there was a report that a woman was killed by a grizzly bear."

"Really?" Olivia said. They now had her full attention. "What happened?"

"Her husband said they were hiking and the bear popped out of nowhere and charged at her. He said they were on their honeymoon, and were supposed to go to Puerto Vallarta, but there was a hurricane, so they decided to go camping instead."

Olivia made a small noise, something between a gasp and a squeak.

"But . . . when did it happen?" she asked.

"Just this morning." Her father looked at Olivia quizzically and smiled. "I wouldn't worry too much, Sweetpea. You're not likely to run into a grizzly in New York City."

"Although"—Mrs. Gribitz put up her finger warningly—"last week there was a report that a woman was bitten on the leg by a ninety-seven-pound squirrel in Hackensack, New Jersey."

THIRTEEN

It was a puzzle. And Olivia was never too fabulous at figuring out puzzles. She found that the more she tried to solve it, the more knotty the puzzle became. As she lay in bed that night, the mystery of the grizzly bear and the play in the Stygian Theater only grew more and more mysterious. How was it possible? How could the play have been about something that hadn't even happened yet? She thought about it until her brain felt hot. She threw off her blanket and blinked into the darkness, listening to her father snoring in the room across the hall. He had come home late that afternoon, much to Olivia's delight. And, since Ansel wasn't around to whisk him off to a parade, he began to tinker with the downstairs toilet, which had been making funny gurgling noises lately.

"Are you sure that's a good idea, Dad?" Olivia had asked nervously. She didn't know if she wanted him to be fired from the brownstone anymore.

"Why not? It's not rocket science, after all," he'd said cheerfully, and she had nodded and smiled at him a little uneasily.

There was no way Olivia was going to be able to sleep—her mind was too muddled. She got out of bed and went to the window, making sure to tiptoe since Ansel's mother was sleeping in the room directly below. She had arrived from Paris that afternoon, while Olivia was at St. Sebastian's, and according to Nora had gone straight to bed with a bad case of jet lag.

Olivia threw open the window that faced the front of the house and leaned out. The street was dark, except for smattered patches of light cast by the streetlamps. A car turned up from Amsterdam Avenue, and as it drove by, its headlight momentarily illuminated a pale figure hunkered on the bottom step of the brownstone. Olivia leaned over farther to get a better look, but the car had passed and the steps were dark again. Still, she could make out a dark shape on the stairs. It wasn't moving. Maybe it was a homeless person who was sleeping on the stairs. Olivia instantly thought of the red-haired man, whom she thought had been asleep on that bench, but had really been dead. A warm, sickish feeling oozed into her belly.

Drawing back into her room, she opened the closet and

pulled out her knapsack. She unzipped the top–it hadn't been unzipped since the last day of school–and sifted through its contents until she found an item that would do the trick–a stale green gumball. She went back to the window and took aim, then lobbed the gumball at the figure below. The gumball landed on the sidewalk rather than the step, but it was enough. The figure jumped up and ran to the top of the stairs. Under the little lamp above the door, the figure was visible–long, pale blond hair, a long white dress, bare feet.

"A ghost!" Olivia said under her breath. Although she'd seen a ghost before, it had not been quite this *ghostly*. She felt a thin chill creep across her skin. She held her breath and kept very still, suddenly terrified of being seen. But the pale figure gazed up, her eyes searching the windows of the brownstone and finally landing on Olivia. She stared at her, then awkwardly raised her hand in greeting. It was this gesture that gave away her identity.

"Dijon!" Olivia called down, keeping her voice as quiet as possible. "What are you doing down there?"

"I . . . I'm . . . I'm here to see Ansel," Dijon said.

"Don't be an idiot, Dijon!" Olivia said. "You're going to get into trouble with Ms. Bender!"

"I don't care," Dijon said.

What a dope! Olivia thought. She reminded herself to never develop a crush on someone–it made you do all kinds of embarrassing things.

"Wait right there," Olivia said. She threw on her robe and a pair of sneakers and rushed down the stairs. At the base of the stairs she jumped into a boat (it was amazing how quickly she had gotten used to traveling on water) and rowed quickly through the canal and into the lagoon.

Outside, Dijon was sitting on the top step, her head buried in her arms. The white dress, Olivia could now see, was really her nightgown, and Dijon's thick, frizzy hair was dyed blond.

"Aw, Dijon, what did you go and dye your hair for?" Olivia couldn't help saying. Dijon looked up. Even her eyebrows were dyed blond. It looked ridiculous on her, as though she'd stuck her whole head in a bowl of flour.

"*I* didn't dye it," she said miserably. "Ms. Bender did. I'm supposed to meet the Vondychomps tomorrow."

"Oh. I'm sorry."

Dijon shrugged. "It don't matter."

"*Doesn't* matter," Olivia said gently.

"Doesn't, don't . . . whatever. They can dye my hair

fourteen-karat freaking gold, I ain't going to fool no one, let's face it. It's hopeless. I ain't like my sister. No one is going to believe that I'm the kid of some countess. Once them Vondychomps meet me, they'll send us all packing back to the Bronx. And then what? Mom will be crushed! She's got her hopes set on this! Plus, she used up every penny she had to send us to Ms. Bender's, and she's in debt up to her ears, and she even sold all her dog-grooming equipment, down to the last flea-and-tick shampoo. We'll be ruined, and all because of me."

"Come on, Dijon, you'll do okay," Olivia tried to reassure her. But inside she was thinking that Dijon was right. In a million years no one would believe that she was one of those pony-riding, *what, what*-saying prep school kids.

"Stop calling me Dijon!" she cried, and stood up. "I'm sick of being called Dijon! My name is *Stacy*." She tipped up her head, pressed her lips together, and blinked rapidly two or three times.

"That's funny," Olivia said.

"What's funny?" Stacy said, the anger still simmering in her voice.

"The way your expression looks right now . . . you remind me of the Princepessa Christina Lilli."

"Who's that?"

"She's royalty. A princess. That's even higher than a countess's daughter."

"Go on," she said disbelievingly. Stacy narrowed her eyes at Olivia, and her head dipped down once again.

"You just lost it, *Dijon,*" Olivia taunted.

"I told you, my name is Stacy!" Stacy jutted her chin out combatively.

"And now it's back again. See, you can do this, Stacy! The Princepessa never says *what, what,* and she doesn't have a pony, and she eats at a crummy little restaurant in the basement of a wig shop. But she has *attitude.* They can't teach that at Ms. Bender's school. You have to be born with it."

"And you think I got attitude, like her?" Stacy was trying unsuccessfully to suppress a smile.

"Right down to your toes," Olivia said. "Just remember that your name is Stacy. Now go back inside before Ms. Bender catches you."

Stacy nibbled her bottom lip as she considered. She glanced at the brownstone door, and Olivia felt sure she was going to ignore her advice and run inside to see Ansel again. Instead, she turned and gave Olivia a friendly shove against her shoulder.

"Thanks," Stacy said, and she started down the stairs, her head held a little higher than usual.

From above, Olivia heard the sound of clapping. She looked up and saw an elderly lady standing on the brownstone's third-floor balcony. The woman wore a green silk dressing gown capped with a tremendous tuft of pink feathers around its collar. The feathers fluted around her face, so that her head looked like an egg hiding in high grass. An egg with tomato-red hair set in curlers.

"Bravo, Olivia Kidney! Well done, darling!" the elderly woman cried.

Olivia stared. Then she smiled. "Madame Brenda!" It was the famous psychic medium whom Olivia had met in her last apartment building. Where had she come from?

Madame Brenda leaned over the balcony, her fuzzy pink slippers peeking through the railing. "It took you exactly ten minutes to do it, darling. Ten minutes! I'm sure that's a record of some sort."

"*What* did I do in ten minutes?" Olivia asked.

"Saved that child's life!"

"Who? Dijon–I mean Stacy?" Olivia glanced back at Stacy, hoping she hadn't heard her, but Stacy was gone. Odd. How had she gotten back into the school so quickly?

"Yes, darling. That little nincompoop was determined to kill herself. She'd been toying with the idea for days, and tonight she meant business."

"I think she just wanted to see Ansel. She has a crush on him."

"Of course she does! Who doesn't have a crush on my handsome son? But that's not why she was here, darling. Come upstairs. I'm getting a pain in the kishkes from this railing."

FOURTEEN

Madame Brenda greeted Olivia with a powerful hug, nearly smothering her in pink feathers. Then she held Olivia out at arm's length and said, "Let me look at you, cupcake. Ah, you are coming into your own, I can see it in your eyes now. In another few years Olivia Kidney will be a force to be reckoned with in the Spirit World!" Madame Brenda pinched Olivia's cheek, then, examining her face more closely, she tut-tutted. "But in the meantime, we must clean out those pores, pronto. Blackheads, whiteheads . . . oh, darling, your skin is a nightmare."

Madame Brenda opened a suitcase and pulled out a pink leather bag. She unzipped it and turned it upside down on the bed. Out tumbled lipsticks, hand creams, miniature soaps, and various plastic bottles and tubes of assorted shapes and colors, all of which Madame Brenda began to sort through.

Olivia sat down on Madame Brenda's bed. "Don't you think this is a weird coincidence, Madame Brenda?"

"Coincidence, my heinie." Madame Brenda opened a tube and squeezed it. A blob of purple goop came out. "Oh yes, this is the stuff. I bought it in Paris last week—a business trip, but it is a positive crime to go to Paris and not do a *little* shopping. I was called there to contact a ghost that was haunting the Louvre museum. The ghost had been rattling a certain oil painting, setting off the alarms and generally being a no-goodnik. So I had a little tête-à-tête with the spirit. It turns out the painting she was rattling was a portrait of her, back in 1659. She didn't like it. She thought it made her nose look too big. I told her that these days people's noses are quite a bit bigger than when she was a girl, so by today's standards, she has a perfect nose. That seemed to satisfy her, and she stopped bothering the painting. But to be brutally honest, she did have a rather big schnoz." She pushed Olivia's hair behind her ears, then began to smear the purple goop on her face.

"It's cold!" Olivia drew back.

"We must suffer for beauty, darling." And she resumed spreading it on Olivia's face. "Now, tell me honestly. Have you been stomping around this house like a three-hundred-pound man in clogs?"

Where had she heard that before? Olivia frowned. She felt the goop hardening on her face.

"It was you who wrote that card!" Olivia exclaimed, suddenly remembering the birthday card that was left on her night table.

"Stop moving your mouth, you'll make the mask crack. Do you feel your pores tightening, darling?"

"I feel like my face is getting sucked off my skull," Olivia said through a grimace.

"Excellent. You'll thank me afterward."

"And I'm guessing I can also thank you for slipping that note under our door at the other apartment." Olivia was beginning to understand how they had wound up at Ansel's in the first place. "So . . . who told you that my dad was an extraordinarily talented handyman?"

"Oh, goodness, no one, darling. Put a wrench in that man's hand and he's an absolute menace!"

"Then why did you hire him?" Olivia asked. Well, really, her face was so stiff by now that it came out: "Weeona-dee-doo-hee-him?" She had to repeat it three times before Madame Brenda understood.

"Oh, it wasn't really your father I was hiring, darling. It was *you.*"

"Me?" Olivia cracked the mask around her lips. "To do what?"

"To do what you were born to do." Madame Brenda quickly patched the cracked mask with some more goop. "Which clearly does not include receiving facials. Now"—Madame Brenda put the top back on the tube—"off to bed." She gave Olivia a dismissive wave of her hand. Olivia stood, then started to ask another question.

"Not another word, cupcake. And don't wash that mask off until morning!"

FIFTEEN

In the morning, the canal water was especially choppy and the current was running fast. As Olivia descended the stairs, carrying Jezebel under her arm, she saw Madame Brenda floating past in an overstuffed armchair, looking irritated and holding a cup of tea at arm's length so that it wouldn't spill on her.

"Good morning, darling," she said as she passed, and she swiftly disappeared down a twist in the canal.

A moment later Ansel floated past, reclining on a couch, also holding a cup of tea. "Take care. Rough seas this morning. The toilet started running and it's churning up the water." And then he too disappeared down the curve.

Other things swirled by—a coffee table, a bookcase, the bathtub, and finally Olivia's father, clinging to the bathroom sink like a Jet Ski as it rode the currents, looking a little sheepish. "Morning, Sweetpea!" he called as he passed by.

Olivia stared at the moored boats bobbing up and down violently. She thought about the snapping turtles that were lurking in the depths, waiting for someone to fall in so they could snap off their toes.

Carefully, she put Jezebel aboard a boat, then stepped in and tentatively untied the mooring rope. The moment the boat was loose, it took off like a dog that had broken its chain and went whirling down the canal, the current spinning it this way and that. Olivia tried to grab the oars, but she was thrown from one side of the boat to the other, until finally she gave up and just clung to Jezebel. It seemed like the current was taking her in the right direction–she just hoped that she wouldn't get smashed to bits on the way. The boat entered the narrow tunnel before the lagoon and slammed hard against one wall, then the other, nearly tipping over altogether. Olivia closed her eyes and held her breath, and suddenly the boat stopped ricocheting and was bobbing a little more gently. Opening her eyes, she saw that she was in the lagoon, as were George, Ansel, and Madame Brenda, who looked very put out but still had managed not to spill her tea.

"Everyone all right?" Ansel asked cheerfully.

"By any chance, George, darling," Madame Brenda asked, "have you been tinkering with the toilet?"

"Well, maybe a little," George admitted.

"Best not to do that again," Madame Brenda advised.

Outside it was threatening to rain. The sky was the color of granite and there was a squally wind blowing. Not great skateboarding weather, but Olivia didn't care. Tomorrow was her field trip with Christopher, and she wanted to surprise him with an ollie.

The park was not as busy as usual. The weather had chased away the joggers and bicyclists, but the skateboarders were at the band shell in full force. In fact, they seemed to be in the middle of a competition. They had set up some fancy ramps made of wood that was curved in the middle and had metal pipes running along the top edges. One skinny kid in a backward baseball cap was skating up a ramp, balancing for a second along the metal rim at the top, then shooting back down. Some of the skateboarders clapped, while others looked a little bored.

Olivia stood off to the side, far enough away not be noticed. Ruben was there, wearing his usual hat jammed down on his head, practicing off on the sidelines.

The skinny kid in the baseball cap shot up and down the ramps a few more times before his board slipped out from under him, and he slid down his final ramp on his backside.

"Oooh," said some of the people in the crowd. The boy picked up his board a little dejectedly and joined the rest of the crowd, some of whom patted him on the back consolingly. Olivia watched as another skateboarder was called up. He rode the ramps easily, and Olivia watched his feet, trying to figure out how he was doing each trick, but he did it so fast, it was hard to tell. He finished his run to a loud round of applause from the spectators.

Then Ruben's name was called. He adjusted his hat and skated toward the ramps. The crowd seemed to be paying more attention now, and Olivia could feel a rising wave of excitement. She moved in closer.

The wind had picked up and the sky was growing darker. All around them the trees were rustling. Some of the skateboarders gazed anxiously up at the sky, but Ruben seemed impervious. He skated up one ramp and came back down and onto the ramp facing it, slow and easy at first. But then he began to pick up speed, his board reaching higher and higher until, at the top edge of the ramp, he leapt up, one hand gripping his board as he was suspended in the air. He skated differently than the other skateboarders—even Olivia could see that. His movements were graceful and fearless, like a quick young cat. Under Ruben's feet, the board seemed like a living thing, reluctant to be separated from him for even a split second. As Olivia watched, her foot pressed down on Jezebel, rolling her back and forth. Under Olivia's feet Jezebel was just a slab of wood with wheels.

Ruben finished, and the crowd started clapping wildly and whistling and thumping him on his back. He flipped his board up with the toe of his sneaker so that it landed in his arms, and walked directly up to Olivia. A light rain had started falling, and the other skateboarders grabbed up their boards and took shelter under the trees.

"You didn't clap," he said accusingly. Olivia looked at him for a moment, blinking quickly to ward off the rain from her eyes.

"I was thinking," she said.

"Can't you clap and think at the same time, Einstein?"

"Everyone else was clapping, so why do you need me to clap?" Olivia replied tartly. "Are you that conceited?" The rain started coming harder now, and a few of the skateboarders hurriedly began to dismantle the ramps.

"I don't care if *they* clap!" Ruben raised his voice, partly to be heard above the rain. "I wanted *you* to clap!" He glared at her, then grabbed his hat off his head and jammed it down on hers. "Come on, you're getting wet!" He grabbed her hand and began to run. The last time a boy had grabbed her hand, it had been Branwell. It had felt different from this.

They ran over to the band shell, up the stairs, and beneath the shelter of the stone arch. They sat down on the stage while the rain pounded against the arch and spilled off its edge in wide, glistening sheets, making Olivia feel that a curtain had fallen, hiding her and Ruben from everyone else in Central Park.

"You're really good," Olivia said, nodding to his skateboard.

"I know it," he said.

Olivia was about to accuse him of being conceited again, but he was right, after all.

"My brother used to be a good skateboarder," Olivia said, taking off Ruben's hat and handing it back to him. "Really, really good."

Ruben nodded. "That's his board then? Jezebel?"

"Yeah." She picked Jezebel up and turned her over. "See that?" She pointed to the blue footprints by the wheels. "Those are mine."

"Man, you have some crazy little feet."

"Mine from when I was younger, genius." Olivia smiled.

"He put them there so you'd be standing on the board with him," Ruben said.

"That's right!" Olivia said, surprised. "How did you know that?"

He shrugged. "Just makes sense. So, your brother doesn't skateboard anymore?"

Olivia shook her head. "He's busy with other things now." Ruben nodded, and there was something about the way he just accepted her explanation that made her feel sort of guilty.

"Well, to tell you the truth," she said, "my brother is dead."

Ruben raised his eyebrows a little. He looked out into the rain, which was beginning to let up, while picking at a scab on his knee. "So what were you thinking about?" he asked. "When you weren't clapping?"

"I was thinking . . . I was thinking that I'm not much of a skateboarder."

"You're really pretty bad at it," Ruben agreed.

"I know I am," Olivia said, already beginning to get annoyed with him again.

"I'm just saying."

"And," Olivia said quickly to shut him up, "I was also thinking that Jezebel deserves to be ridden by someone

who *is* a good skateboarder. And since my brother can't ride her anymore . . ." She put Jezebel on his lap.

He looked down at the board, and then at Olivia. "Really?" he asked incredulously.

Olivia nodded, fighting off last-minute regrets.

"Wow! That is a really, really—"

"Yeah, yeah." Olivia waved it off.

"—a really, really intelligent thing to do, because you were about to break your neck the way you were riding her."

Olivia glared at him. The rain outside had stopped, and the sky was beginning to lighten.

"Tell you what." He handed her his old skateboard. "Take mine." Then he picked up Jezebel and slid off the band shell stage. "And come by the park tomorrow afternoon. I'll give you your first lesson."

Olivia watched as he skated away on Jezebel. She had a small spasm of jealousy, but then she looked down at his board in her hands. She bit her lip, trying to hold back a smile.

The storm was gone as quickly as it had arrived, and the sun was pushing out through the gloom, glinting against the puddles. Olivia jumped off the band shell—landing a little clumsily, unlike Ruben. The ground was too wet to practice on now, but the sun was so strong, the ground would be dry enough in no time.

She ambled through the park to kill time. When she got hungry, she bought a hot dog from a vendor, along with a small bag of potato chips and a soda. She found an empty bench and looked around to make sure no one was watching her. Then she put the bag of chips on the bench and sat down on them, stood up and sat down on them again, and then once more, just to be thorough. Then she ripped the bag open and carefully shook the crushed chips onto her hot dog. She knew it was weird, but since she was a little kid she had always eaten her hot dogs like that. And it was probably the best way to eat a hot dog, in any case.

The sun felt all melty and nice on her shoulders as she sat nibbling away and looking at Ruben's skateboard. She thought about Ruben. He wasn't at all like Branwell. Not nearly as nice. But she kind of liked him anyway. She hoped Branwell didn't think she was forgetting about him. She wasn't, not at all. It's just that sometimes it was hard to keep him in her mind.

She suddenly thought about the girl in the coma. How the hospital volunteer had said that her relatives seemed to have forgotten about her. At least Branwell had company where he was—Christopher said the afterlife was as bustling as Grand Central Station. But that girl was all alone inside her body. Neither dead nor alive. It must be awful, Olivia thought. And today is her birthday.

The idea came to Olivia in an instant: I should visit her! Just to tell her happy birthday. Just so she knows someone other than the nurses is thinking about her. The more she thought about it, the faster she ate her hot dog, so that a little kid passing by pushed up her nose and oinked at Olivia. Olivia stuck her tongue out at the girl—something she hadn't done since she was seven—popped the rest of her hot dog in her mouth, grabbed Ruben's skateboard, and set off determinedly for St. Sebastian's.

The East Wing of St. Sebastian's was livelier than usual. Voices and laughter were bubbling up through the hallways, and several nurses walked through the halls with smiles on their faces. The door to the girl's room was ajar today. The room was festooned with balloons and streamers, and though the girl's screen was still drawn, it was decorated with cards.

"Can I help you?" asked a nurse who was coming up the hall.

"I'm here to visit a patient," Olivia said.

"And the patient's name?" the nurse asked.

“It’s her.” Olivia pointed to the girl’s room. “I’m here to see her.”

The nurse could not have looked more surprised. “Really? Well . . . that’s wonderful! Are you a member of her family?”

“No. Just a friend.”

“Wonderful! Yes, go ahead, go on in,” the nurse said, and she continued down the hall.

Olivia stood at the door’s threshold. She could hear the steady sound of breathing. But it wasn’t a human sound. It was too loud and regular and hollow-sounding. She focused on the girl’s feet, since the rest of her was hidden by the screen, and a queasy dread rose up in her. Suppose the girl was grotesquely disfigured. Maybe that’s why they kept the screen there. Maybe that was why no one wanted to visit her. The more Olivia listened to the breathing, the more she thought it had a monstrous sound to it.

I can’t do it, Olivia thought. I just can’t. I don’t want to look at her. Olivia turned to go, when she heard a squealing noise. Swinging around the opposite end of the hallway was the volunteer from the other day. She recognized Olivia instantly.

“Hello, hello! Back again?”

“Yeah. I’m here to see my dad,” Olivia lied. She nodded

shyly at the girl's room. "Did . . . did she have a good birthday?"

"Oh, sure she did! We even had a cake. One of the nurses blew out the candle and made a wish *for* her. Of course we all knew what it was."

"What was it?"

"Well," the volunteer had lowered her voice conspiratorially, "yesterday afternoon, she moved her toe. Just the tiniest bit."

"Oh. Is that important?" Olivia asked.

"Important? It's a little bit of a miracle! We're all keeping our fingers crossed for her. You keep yours crossed too." The volunteer said good-bye and jauntily clattered off with her cart.

Olivia looked into the room at the girl's toes. They were perfectly still. Yet Olivia could imagine them moving—the tiniest little twitch—as if to tell people that she was alive in there somewhere, and that she was listening.

Warily, Olivia stepped into the room. The eerie breathing grew louder, making Olivia feel a little gluey in her stomach, but she forced herself to keep going. Now she could see the girl's hand lying at her side. Someone had painted her nails a soft peach color. It looked like a normal hand, not scarred or disfigured, but her wrists were very thin.

Taking a deep breath, Olivia stepped past the screen and directly up to the bed. She let her eyes move up the girl's body, so thin and frail beneath the cotton hospital gown. A tube was inserted into her left arm and attached to a plastic bag hanging from a tall metal stand. Slowly, Olivia's eyes drifted up to the girl's face. Olivia cried out, then put her hand to her mouth to stifle the noise. The face was thinner, the skin had an ashen cast, and a tube was inserted into her mouth and attached to a machine that was making the strange breathing noise. But despite all that, there was no mistaking it.

"Nora." She stared down into the still, quiet face, the closed eyelids with their slightly purplish hue. It was Nora's face, but with all the wild, pulsating energy gone.

Olivia felt her breathing quicken, and an old fear—one that she thought she had seen the last of—now returned full force: Maybe I'm crazy, Olivia thought. Maybe I see things that aren't there. I talk to my brother, and my brother is dead. Isn't that a sign that I'm crazy? Maybe this is too. Her thoughts wound around themselves in a panicked tangle. She looked at Nora again. I could be wrong, she thought. Maybe this isn't Nora at all. Maybe this person only looks like her.

She remembered the birthday cards taped up on the

screen, and quickly went around to the other side. She opened one with a picture of a mouse wearing a birthday hat. Inside it said, *To my favorite patient. Happy Birthday, Nora! Love, Doctor Joseph.* She opened another one that said, *To Nora, Happy Birthday. We love you! The East Wing nurses.*

She shook her head—it made no sense. How could it be? A card taped up to the corner of the screen, set apart from the others, caught her eye. The card had a picture of the night sky on its front, with stars raised up in shiny bits of foil. Olivia opened it up. *Happy Birthday, Uncle!* was printed inside. Underneath it said:

> Dear Olivia,
>
> Didn't I tell you not to jump to conclusions? Yes, darling, you have stumbled upon something. You are confused, perplexed, vashtumped. And what does one do when one is vashtumped? One shops for shoes, of course! Meet me at Bloomingdale's, fourth floor, at 3:30. And don't forget to tell Nora happy birthday. She does hear you—every word.

Madame Brenda. She knew the answer to this; she was at the heart of all of this, Olivia was certain! She looked at her watch. It was 3:05. Bloomingdale's was on 59th Street, so she'd have to hurry. She went back to Nora's bedside and looked down at her, then let her hand graze the top of Nora's hand. She had thought it would feel cold, but no, it was warm. She put her hand over Nora's and squeezed it gently.

"Happy birthday, Nora," Olivia said.

Sixteen

Bloomingdale's was brightly lighted and crowded and confusing. Olivia was bumped and jostled through the crowds, craning her neck trying to find the escalators as she inched past counters of cosmetics and perfumes and watches and handbags. Leggy, lipsticked women were spraying people with perfumes, making Olivia woozy from the mishmash of smells. Finally, off to her right she spotted the escalator going up. Skirting through a cluster of German tourists, she made her way to the escalator and rode it up to the fourth floor. She liked escalators. When I grow up, I'm going to live in an apartment with an escalator, she thought dreamily, still feeling a little tipsy from the perfumes.

On the fourth floor she found the shoe department, and from there it wasn't hard to find Madame Brenda. She was dressed in an acid green tank top and red culottes and was walking back and forth unsteadily in a pair of blue, very high-heeled sandals with a gigantic orange butterfly on the toe strap, while a slim, balding young man in a suit watched her. When she saw Olivia, she toddled over to her.

"So?" She stuck her leg out and twisted her ankle back and forth. "What do you think? What's your impression?"

Olivia shrugged. "I don't know. I guess they're kind of ugly."

"Really?" Madame Brenda sounded surprised and turned to look at the man in the suit. "My friend says they're ugly."

The man looked Olivia up and down disdainfully, taking in her wet clothes and her skateboard. "Perhaps your friend cannot tell the difference between ugly and stylishly daring."

"I know ugly when I see it," Olivia shot back at him.

"Ugly it is, then," Madame Brenda proclaimed, and she removed the sandals and held them out to the man, who took them churlishly. "Come, let's see what else they've got."

In her stockinged feet she strolled over to a shelf of even higher-heeled sandals and began to examine them.

"Madame Brenda," Olivia began, "that really was Nora, then? In the hospital?"

"Oh yes, that was her," she said, picking up a silver sandal with purple sparkles on it and a see-through heel. "Sad to see her in that state, isn't it? She's such a lively girl in the house."

"But how can it be?" Olivia asked.

"It *shouldn't* be," Madame Brenda said with sudden heat in her voice. "It is against all the rules!" She put the silver sandal down and picked up a pair of black leather sandals with very long straps that tied up the leg. "But when has Ansel ever followed the rules, especially when it spoils his own fun? He's not a bad boy, mind you. He's very good at what he does. But he's completely undisciplined."

"What *does* he do?" Olivia asked.

"Why, he teaches people how to die, darling." Madame Brenda hailed the slim salesman and waved the leather sandal at him. "Size eight, extra wide!" she called to him and then said to Olivia in an aside, "I'd be a regular wide if it weren't for my bunions."

"But . . . but people don't have to learn how to die," Olivia objected.

"And how would you know?"

Olivia guessed she had a point. She was silent for a minute, then asked, "You mean all those people that come at night? . . ."

"Yes, all about to die. Ansel runs what is called an Exit Academy. People come to him for lessons while they're dreaming. Their bodies are still in bed, darling, but their spirits are traveling. Your friend Stacy had been taking lessons with Ansel for the past week, even though Ansel had been trying like mad to talk her out of it."

"But if Dijon–I mean, if Stacy was only dreaming, how come I saw her standing right in front of me?"

"It's a puzzle, isn't it? And here's your answer: the brownstone is located on what's called a 'spirit hot spot'– a simple matter of longitude and latitude. Spirits have more density there, so you can actually see them. There are other Exit Academies all over the world, and they're all located on hot spots just like that one."

The salesman emerged from a back room carrying a shoe box. Madame Brenda took a seat, and the salesman knelt beside her to put the sandals on her feet, but she dismissed him with a wave of her hand.

"I can put my own shoes on, thank you. I've been doing it since I was four." The salesman grimaced in a way that was supposed to be a smile.

"What sort of things do Exit Academies teach people?" Olivia asked as Madame Brenda tied the long straps in crisscrosses up her calf.

"Oh, lots of things. But you'll find out soon enough."

Olivia's eyes grew wide. "Do you mean I'm going to–?"

"Die? Oh, goodness no, darling, not for many, many years yet!" She stood up and walked back and forth to try out the sandals. "However, I do need your help. I was hoping to find someone a little older, of course, with a little more experience in these matters–it's a tricky business and there is a teensy-weensy bit of danger. But there wasn't anyone else, darling–what?!" Madame Brenda turned suddenly to the salesman, who was hanging around, looking impatient.

"The sandals, ma'am?"

"They make me feel like I have snakes crawling up my legs." She untied the straps and handed the sandals back to the salesman, who practically snatched them out of her hands. Madame Brenda put her own shoes back on and said, "Come, let's go upstairs and have a little snack, and I'll explain things better."

They took the escalator up to the seventh floor and sat at the store's little café. Madame Brenda ordered a pot of tea and a plate of cookies, which the waitress brought promptly, along with tiny blue teacups for both of them. The cookies were frosted pink and shaped like an elephant's tusk. Madame Brenda poured the tea, and stirred five teaspoons of sugar into her own cup before taking a sip.

"Now," said Madame Brenda, "one of the things an Exit Academy does is rehearse people's moment of death with them. So it won't come as a shock. If they're calm, they can pass more easily. Each person is given their own script, and they rehearse their death the same way you'd rehearse a play, with sets and actors and a script."

Olivia thought of Lillian's play, *Into the Woods . . . For Good.* And the next day Lillian had been attacked by a grizzly bear. She must have been rehearsing her death in the Stygian Theater.

"Now, it's these scripts that I am most concerned about. They're enormously important. They are, in fact, the key to passing in the safest and most correct way. Ansel keeps all the scripts locked up in a vault. Including Nora's script." Madame Brenda dipped the pointy end of a cookie into her tea and bit off the tip.

"Nora went to Ansel's academy?" Olivia asked.

"About ten months ago. She was in an accident. She was riding a motorcycle, going much too fast, as usual, and she lost control and crashed into a guardrail. She was alive when they found her, oh, but barely, darling, barely. They took her to the hospital. No one expected her to survive. And she herself was ready to die. So she came to Ansel to learn how to do it. But Ansel . . . grew fond of her. *Too* fond of her. And he didn't want to let her go. You must understand that my son has a most difficult job, maybe the most difficult job of all. He is a young man, full of life, and yet he spends his time around dying people. Then along comes Nora—lively and full of fun—so like him—and he couldn't bring himself to let her go. So he kept her script as a way to stall for more time with her, never allowing her in the vault to see it. And the longer she stayed at the brownstone, the dimmer her memory became, until she forgot why she even came in the first place. That can happen when the spirit is away from the body for too long. Now she's stuck in the brownstone, unable to go outside."

"But she went outside yesterday," Olivia said.

"And then she felt ill and had to go back in, true? She's lost, darling. She's neither dead nor alive. She is trapped. And Nora is a girl who likes to be free. Slowly, bit by bit, her spirit is becoming frayed and weak, and soon it will snap, like a piece of old string."

"What will happen to her then?"

"She'll drift off, away from the brownstone, out into the world without knowing why. She'll wander the earth confused, lost, and alone. Much like your friend Branwell used to."

At the mention of Branwell, Olivia felt a sharp ache of

pity. She remembered the sadness in his voice when he admitted to always longing for something he couldn't name.

Olivia looked down at her tea, which was growing cold without her having touched a drop of it. She shook her head slowly. "Well, I don't see how I'm supposed to help."

Madame Brenda glanced around at the other tables, then leaned in closer to Olivia. "You, Olivia, are what is called a Straddler. It's very rare. It happens only once in a blue moon. The last Straddler was a goat herder in the second century B.C. A Straddler, darling, is a living person who has one foot on earth and the other in the Spirit World. That's why it is so easy for you to chat with your delightful brother. True, I can also speak with the dead, but as a Straddler, you have abilities that far exceed my own. A Straddler is even *built* differently than other people."

Olivia thought of all the weird things about her body—her fingers always seemed too long for her hands, and her tongue had a little bump on it, toward the back, and no matter how often she cleaned behind her ears there was always this smear of yellowish stuff on the Q-tip.

"Your *spirit* is built differently," Madame Brenda added, seeing Olivia's face turn red. "Ansel noticed it right away. He asked me yesterday if I sensed death was close for you. I told him yes, I most certainly sensed it."

"Why did you tell him that?!" Olivia cried.

"I told him that, darling, because I need you to enroll in the Exit Academy. If you pretend to be a person who has come for lessons, your spirit is sufficiently light to make it believable. I, for instance, would be detected immediately as a fraud. As a student, you'll be given access to the Script Vault, where you'll be able to fetch Nora's script."

Olivia hesitated. "You said something about it being dangerous."

"I said a 'teensy-weensy bit of danger.' There are . . . some odd birds that hang around Exit Academies. Mostly just eccentric spirits, perfectly harmless. But on occasion you can run into a spirit that means to do some harm. They'll be naturally attracted to you, since you have a foot in both worlds."

"How can I tell if they mean harm or are just eccentric?"

"I knew you'd ask that question. And unfortunately, I don't have a very good answer. All I can say is that if you see a spirit that just gives you the heebie-jeebies, keep clear of it."

"By *harm,* do you mean they could actually kill me?" Olivia asked.

Madame Brenda held up her thumb and her pointer

finger so that there was a small space between them. "Tiny chance." She took a sip of her tea, and added, "In order to swallow your soul."

"Are you kidding me?" This whole business was beginning to look more and more disagreeable.

"You must understand, for a spirit who can't accept death, a Straddler's soul is extremely valuable, cupcake," Madame Brenda explained. "Swallowing the average, run-of-the-mill human soul is totally useless. I know a few spirits who've tried. They say the darn thing flops and wriggles around inside you like a salmon out of water, and is so generally annoying that they finally let it go. The average soul can't survive on earth after the body dies, at least not in the same way. Its rightful home is in the Spirit World. But a Straddler's soul–oh, cupcake, that is a whole different story! A Straddler's soul can exist on the earth and in the Spirit World at the same time. It is like one of those creatures that can live in the water *and* on the land–an ambilicord?"

"Amphibian," Olivia said. "But what exactly would they try and do with my soul?"

Madame Brenda hesitated. She poured herself more tea from the pot, stirred five more spoonfuls of sugar into her cup. "Nothing very nice, I'm afraid. After they swallow your soul, they would shove themselves right back into your body. You would live, darling, but, I won't lie to you, you'd be in a sorry little pickle. Your body would be at their mercy. They could do what they liked with you, against your will, and let me tell you these types of spirits often have one or two screws loose."

Olivia frowned and shook her head. "I don't think I want to do this."

Madame Brenda replaced her cup in its saucer and dabbed at the corners of her mouth with her napkin. "Perfectly understandable." She raised her hand to call over the waitress. "Check, please."

SEVENTEEN

During dinner–which George cooked and which everyone, even Nora, agreed was the best meal they'd ever had in the house–Olivia sat distractedly picking at her food. Olivia found she was reluctant to look at Nora. For one thing, it reminded her of the still, pitiful Nora at St. Sebastian's. And for another–well, she felt guilty.

"Are you all right, Olivia?" George asked.

"I'm fine," Olivia said. "Just not that hungry. I think I'm going to go up to my room."

"But there's chocolate mousse for dessert," George said.

"Let the child go, George," Madame Brenda said. "She looks like she has a lot on her mind."

Olivia went up to her room and lay down on her bed. Her mind teetered back and forth, arguing with itself: You shouldn't feel guilty. After all, what Madame Brenda is asking you to do is crazy! You'd be risking your own life! And besides, Nora seems fine just as she is. But another part of her argued back: Nora is *not* fine! She can't even leave the house! Remember how happy she looked when she was riding on Jezebel? Her face was so alive! And Madame Brenda said the danger was "teensy-weensy" . . . Her thoughts went round and round, until she heard a knock on her door.

"Come in," Olivia said wearily.

To Olivia's dismay, it was Nora, holding a bowl of chocolate mousse topped with a mound of whipped cream.

"Thanks," Olivia said, looking up at the ceiling, "but I don't want any."

"Who said it was for you?" Nora sat down on the bed. "Look, I think I know what's bugging you, kid."

Olivia turned and looked at Nora apprehensively.

"I've been noticing a change in you," Nora continued. "You're steadier on your feet. You're not stumbling and weaving around. You don't smell of booze any more. Tell me the truth–you've stopped drinking, haven't you?"

There was really nothing for Olivia to do but nod.

"I knew it!" Nora said. She put her chocolate mousse down on the night table and scooped Olivia into her arms, hugging her tightly. "Now, I know you may not feel too great for the next couple of days. That's normal after you stop drinking. But it will pass, I promise. I'm real proud of you, kid."

Nora let go of Olivia and looked at her intently, smiling. Nora's eyes were brilliant and clear and so full of life. Olivia swallowed back an urge to cry.

"Got to go." Nora stood up. "I promised Ansel's mother I'd let her exfoliate my feet after dinner. I'm sure I'll regret it." She left the room, closing the door softly, leaving Olivia to reconsider, as she took a bite of the mousse that Nora had left, exactly how big a "tiny chance" of death was.

"Fine, okay . . . I'll do it."

Olivia entered Madame Brenda's room that night without knocking. Madame Brenda was sitting on the floor in blue- and red-striped silk pajamas, her legs straight out in front of her while she painted her toenails. She was talking to herself too, and she didn't even stop when Olivia entered. Instead, she held up an "I'll be with you in a moment" finger toward Olivia and continued talking.

"The fact is, I'm sick and tired of your jealousy," Madame Brenda was saying as she carefully brushed polish onto her pinky toe. "The man at the museum was simply making small talk." She paused a moment as if listening and said, "Well, yes, darling, he did tell me I have the ankles of a movie star, but you know how French men are. Now, run along, I have company." Madame Brenda sighed and shook her head at Olivia. "My late husband, Frank. When he was alive he barely paid any attention to me, and now that he's dead the man watches me like a hawk." She put a final stroke on her toe, capped the brush, leaned back on her hands, and scissored her legs back and forth to dry the polish. "Now, what is it you said before?"

"I said I'll do it," Olivia said irritably.

"Of course you will. I never even had a doubt. I've already arranged everything."

This annoyed Olivia, since the decision had not been an easy one.

Madame Brenda patted the floor. "Sit down by me." And while Madame Brenda continued to dry her toes, she explained the plan to Olivia. "Wait until after midnight, then go down to the second floor. And knock, darling, which incidentally you should make a habit of in any case."

"How am I supposed to find Nora's script anyway?" Olivia asked.

"Simple. All the scripts in the vault are alphabetized. Nora's last name is Horn. When you find it, smuggle it out of the academy and bring it back to me."

"But how am I supposed to do that without being caught?" Olivia asked.

"Well, darling, I can't tell you how to do *everything,* can I?"

"You haven't told me how to do *anything!*" Olivia stood up now, furious and wondering how wise it was to listen to Madame Brenda in the first place, but Madame Brenda reached up and quickly grabbed Olivia's hand and squeezed it. "Do you think I would send you if I wasn't ninety-nine point eight percent sure that you will succeed, Olivia?"

It was that .2 percent that made Olivia go into her father's room that evening to say good night, and give him a hug that knocked the wind out of him.

Eighteen

Olivia set her alarm clock for midnight, which really wasn't necessary since she couldn't fall asleep. When the alarm went off, she got up and dressed. She took her toolbox out of the closet and went into Madame Brenda's room, knocking softly before she entered. Madame Brenda was sleeping with a pale blue mask over her eyes, but when Olivia came close, she lifted the mask to the top of her head and whispered, "All good to go, cupcake?"

Olivia nodded. "Could you do me a favor and keep this safe?" Olivia put the toolbox beside Madame Brenda on the bed. Madame Brenda looked at the box curiously.

"May I?" she asked Olivia, pointing to the latch.

"Okay," Olivia said.

Madame Brenda raised herself up on one elbow, flipped open the latch, and looked inside. "Ahh." She nodded. Inside were the brother and sister dolls that looked exactly like Olivia and Christopher. Christopher had believed that, since they looked so much like him and Olivia, they were effigies–which meant that if something bad happened to the dolls, it might also happen to Olivia and Christopher. Consequently, he had kept them tucked away in a safe place. Now they were in Olivia's care.

"I'll guard them like a she-wolf," Madame Brenda assured her.

Olivia went down the stairs to the door on the second floor and knocked softly. She half hoped that no one would hear her, but Ansel opened the door after a minute's wait.

"Oh dear," he said. His handsome face fell, and Olivia saw his throat shift as he swallowed hard. He forced a smile at Olivia. "Well, it seems we have some work to do." His voice sounded odd, sort of the way it sounded on the night that George fell sick. "Come inside, and we'll head on over to the auditorium. You can meet the other newcomers–a nice bunch, yes, a nice bunch," he said distractedly.

Olivia followed Ansel down the hall to an open door on the right-hand side. Inside it looked just like a miniature school auditorium. Three other people were already seated, and Ansel indicated to Olivia that she should sit too. She took a seat on the end of the aisle, away from the others, while Ansel climbed the stairs to a little stage and stood before a microphone.

"Well." Ansel looked at the seated people and clapped his hands. "Looks like the gang's all here. My name is Ansel Plover and I want to welcome you to the Exit Academy. This evening I'll be giving you just a little taste of the things we will be learning in the coming days. You will also be picking up your scripts, which will tell you exactly how you are going to die—something I'm sure you are all most anxious to find out. We have many topics to cover tonight, so I'll ask that you all stay together. If at any time you feel your body might be waking up, raise your hand and I will bring you some warm milk and read passages from an eighth-grade physics textbook to help you fall back to sleep. Any questions?"

A man with a jowly face and a firm potbelly raised his hand.

"Yes, Mr. Hopper?" Ansel said.

"Can I postpone my death until after the World Series?"

"I'm afraid not, my friend. Any other questions?"

An old woman in a yellow fedora raised her hand.

"Yes, Ms. Bosh?"

"My sister died last year. Am I going to see her there?"

"Of course," Ansel said.

"But I can't stand my sister," Ms. Bosh complained.

"Then by all means avoid her," Ansel suggested. "Any other questions?" The room was silent. "No? Excellent. Follow me."

Ansel led the way out of the auditorium and down the hall. Up ahead, clustered together, was a team of football players. As Olivia came closer, she saw that they were only football jerseys on stand-up dummies, complete with helmets and shoulder pads.

"All right," Ansel said, stopping by the dummies. "Choose your uniform."

"Excuse me, but why do we need to wear these things?" asked a tall, prim-looking woman with carefully coiffed red hair.

"It will all become clear in a moment, Ms. Krickle," Ansel assured her.

Olivia chose the smallest uniform—New York Giants—and put on the heavy shoulder pads, lacing it up in front, then the jersey, and finally the helmet, which was a little big for her. She pushed it back so that she could actually see through the visor.

Suddenly there was a *shishhing* sound, and a pair of legs

clad in black heels emerged out of a rectangular plastic flap marked OUT in the wall behind them. Then came the edge of a skirt, topped with a Green Bay Packers jersey, then a helmeted head. The woman staggered to her feet, breathing hard and sticking her arms out to the side to regain her balance.

"Careful. It's wild in there tonight!" she advised the others as she removed her uniform.

"Ready, then?" Ansel said. "All right, you are about to get a taste of what it's like to be without a human body. At the moment you are in a dream state, so you are all a little lighter than usual. However, in the Spirit World you will be as light as a mote of dust. It takes some getting used to, so you'll stay in just for a few minutes–you'll be able to practice more over the next few days. Now I want you to enter the room one at a time for safety's sake, so line up."

Mr. Hopper, the baseball fan, dressed as a Dallas Cowboy, jostled his way to the head of the crowd. To the right of the plastic opening in the wall was a tall metal chute, nearly seven feet high, with a handle attached to it. Ansel pulled the handle and the chute opened from the top, like a giant dishwasher. Inside there was a little place to stand, with a metal bar in front. Ansel unlatched the bar and directed Mr. Hopper to step inside.

"Not going to hurt, is it?" he joked as Ansel replaced the metal bar.

"Only a little," Ansel said, and he closed the chute, muffling the man's sudden objections. There was a *fooosh-ing* sound and a smothered yelp from the man inside, and then silence.

The next person in line was Ms. Bosh, who was not quite so eager now, but Ansel hurried her along inside and closed the chute. Again the *fooosshing* sound came, but no yelp this time, which was somehow even more ominous. Olivia was up next. She stepped into the chute, her stom-ach fluttery, but she was excited too.

"The trick is to relax," Ansel whispered to her before he latched the bar and closed the chute with a metallic clank. With the door closed, her body was tipped forward, the bar keeping her from falling over. Suddenly she felt a tremendous pull from above and *fooosh!* She was sucked up through a short tube and into a big room. *SLAM!* No sooner had she entered the room than Mr. Hopper col-lided with her, hurling her against the wall.

"Sorry about that!" he called to her as he flew by, up-side down.

The wall, it turned out, was padded, and it pulled Olivia back against it as though she were a magnet on a refrigerator. She stayed there for a minute to catch her breath, her legs and arms splayed against the wall. Even though she was five feet or so off the ground, the wall held her securely against it.

The room had several other people floating around in its center, some very gracefully, doing somersaults in the air, then diving down and shooting up while others were flopping around like marionette puppets. After a *foooshing* sound Ms. Krickle shot through the tube's opening in the wall with a screech.

Well, I might as well give it a try, Olivia thought. She pulled her left hand off the wall, and then her right, then her upper body. With her legs still pinned to the wall, her body dipped down as though she were bowing, and she struggled to pull her legs off, but couldn't in that position. One of the more expert people saw her predicament and did a sort of midair backstroke over to her.

"Youse need a hand?" he asked.

"Yes, please," Olivia said.

The man grabbed her wrists and gave a tug. Her legs pulled off from the wall and she was suddenly in midair.

"Hey, you're the kid from the other night," the man said. He was still holding her wrists. "It's me, Louie. The guy with the rotten luck."

"Oh, the man in the white coveralls!" Olivia exclaimed.

"That's right." She could see him smile behind his visor. "Should I let go of you yet?"

Olivia looked around. Everyone else was managing, for better or worse. "I guess so," she said.

Louie let go of her right wrist first, and the whole right side of Olivia's body flung out and flopped around. Then he let go of her left wrist. For a second Olivia hovered in the air, motionless. Then she moved her leg the slightest bit and instantly flew sideways, her shoulder pads crashing against the shoulder pads of Ms. Krickle, the prim red-haired woman, knocking the woman against the wall.

"Sorry," Olivia started to say, but her index finger had twitched in the other direction and she immediately flew that way, until she foolishly looked down and her whole body flipped over so that she was hanging upside down. Mr. Hopper flew by, brushing against her just enough to flip her back, right side up.

She was starting to get it now. You had to be very careful about every muscle in your body, because if any part of you moved even the littlest bit in one direction, that's the way you would fly. She remembered what Ansel had said: "The trick is to relax." Olivia kept still and took a deep breath. She imagined that she was floating in a big swimming pool. Her muscles began to loosen. Then, just to see, she pointed her foot to the left. Her body drifted to the left, but more slowly now, so that she could control it better. She kept breathing deeply and tipped her head back. She easily did a backward somersault. It felt so great that she laughed out loud.

"Hey, there you go! That's the way!" Louie cried, and he slapped her on the back, which startled her. Her muscles tightened again, and she did a crazy zigzagging dance, knocking into several people before slapping against the wall, front first.

She pulled her left hand off the wall and swung it around, then her left leg until she was splayed with her back against the wall, facing forward again. Bit by bit, she managed to pull herself off the wall, and she continued to practice flying in the middle of the room.

When she began to gain her confidence, she glanced around at the others. Ms. Bosh was dog-paddling in quick little scooping movements and flipping herself over and over, but Ms. Krickle wasn't faring very well. She was so stiff that she was ricocheting around the room like a bullet, until she ricocheted right into the OUT chute. Ms. Bosh dog-paddled toward the OUT chute too and disappeared through it. Olivia figured she should probably go through the OUT chute also, even though she was having so much fun, and Mr. Hopper followed.

"How exhilarating!" Ms. Bosh cried, removing her uniform and beaming. "It must be how fish feel!"

Ms. Krickle looked decidedly dazed as she struggled to remove her helmet, so Ansel gave her a hand. He carefully smoothed down her hair, which was standing on end like a well-used broom, then announced, "All right, my friends, gather your wits, collect your thoughts, and come to your senses. You are going to need a healthy dose of all three for our next room!"

NINETEEN

Ansel started back up the hallway until he came to a door marked 38. He put his hand on the knob, turned to them, and said, "Now, we are about to encounter the most disturbing, most alarming, most horrible thing that people encounter in the Spirit World." He looked around at them gravely. "Ready?"

"Well . . . I mean, what are we talking about?" asked Mr. Hopper nervously. "Demons? Goblins? Vampires?"

"Vampires," the red-haired Ms. Krickle snorted derisively.

"Worse," Ansel said. He turned the knob, and Olivia held her breath, bracing herself to flee if necessary. But when Ansel opened the door, she could see nothing but a perfectly empty room. There wasn't even any furniture. Ansel hustled everyone inside, looked at them all, and smiled.

"Enjoy yourselves," he said. He shut the door and

locked it. For a moment no one said anything. They looked around the room nervously.

"I don't like this," Ms. Bosh said.

"And I don't like that stupid fedora you're wearing, but you don't hear me complaining," said Mr. Hopper.

Everyone turned to look at him.

"What?" he said. "Why's everyone staring at me?"

"Because that was rude!" said Ms. Krickle. "Still, that fedora is pretty stupid-looking, I must admit. She looks like a wrinkly mobster."

Ms. Bosh gasped. But Olivia had noticed something bizarre. Ms. Krickle had spoken out loud only when she called Mr. Hopper rude. Her lips hadn't moved during the rest of it.

"I think we must be reading each other's minds," Olivia thought. And everyone turned to look at her, since they heard her think it. Knowing that they could hear her thoughts made her so nervous that she thought the very thing she didn't want them to hear: "I hope no one farts in here—there are no windows."

"Oh, now that's just uncalled for!" Ms. Krickle cried.

"That dame is so uptight, she'd probably explode if she farted," Mr. Hopper thought, and then he said out loud, "Oops." That made Olivia laugh. Mr. Hopper looked at her.

"Poor kid, dying so young," Mr. Hopper thought. Olivia stopped laughing. Mr. Hopper's voice sounded so sad that she couldn't help but think, "I'm not dying, not really. Not actually."

The others' voices all came together in a quiet chorus: "She doesn't know," "She's too young to understand," "Poor kid, poor kid." Ms. Bosh dabbed at her eyes with her thumb. Olivia could feel Ms. Bosh's sadness, feel it in her entire body so powerfully that she too started to cry. She looked around at the others. Now she could feel Mr. Hopper's and Ms. Krickle's sadness too, and she guessed that they could feel hers, and each other's, until the sadness piled up on itself like snow in a blizzard. And although it was so awfully sad, Olivia also felt a kind of bond with everyone in the room, as though they all knew each other much, much better than they actually did, and liked each other immensely.

It was then that Ansel unlocked the door. He was carrying a box of tissues.

"So," said Mr. Hopper, wiping the tears from his cheek, "are you telling me that in the Spirit World everyone hears what everyone else is thinking?"

"That is exactly what I'm telling you," Ansel said, and he held out the box of tissues so everyone could grab a handful.

"How did you know we'd need these?" Ms. Krickle sniffled.

"Oh, the tissues always come in handy–sometimes they're used to mop up tears, and sometimes they're used to mop up bloody noses. I never know which it will be, but it's almost always one or the other."

After eyes had been wiped and noses had been blown, they all backtracked down the hall, following Ansel, until he stopped in front of Room 23.

"Now we come to the Harbingers of Doom Room," Ansel said. "You'll be able to select your harbinger from a handsome selection of birds and insects."

"But what do we need them for?" Olivia asked.

"They'll give you the cue that the time of death is close. You might, for instance, look out your bedroom window and spot an owl staring back at you in a peculiar way, and that will be your clue that you need to prepare for departure–you know, say good-bye to a loved one, feed the cat, comb your hair. Now, lots of people opt for the crows–they're very traditional. But I think the moths have a certain elegance."

He opened the door to Room 23 and a squawking, hooting mayhem immediately erupted. It was the same room Olivia had been in before—the room with all the birds and moths and the pigeon that flew into the windowpane.

Ansel reached into his jacket pocket, pulled out four red tags with string attached to them, and handed one out to everyone. Olivia looked at hers. It had OLIVIA KIDNEY printed on it in bold black letters.

"When you find a harbinger you like, just tie this tag to it. But watch your fingers around the crows, they're a little nippy. When you're finished"—Ansel started back down the hall—"you can meet me in front of Room Forty-two."

After they all entered the room and closed the door, the birds' wild hoots and squawks gradually died down. They shifted on their perches and ruffled their feathers, watching the people with sharp, guarded eyes. Now the room was eerily quiet, except for the occasional loud thump when the white pigeon flew into the windowpane.

"Youch!" Mr. Hopper said each time, on the bird's behalf.

They all began to walk slowly around the room, trying to pick out their harbingers. All of them except Olivia. She had heard a tapping noise on the far end of the room—three taps and then a pause. Another three taps, then a pause. Olivia looked around at the others. No one else had appeared to notice the tapping. Ms. Krickle was standing in front of a particularly snappish-looking crow, holding her hand out to it tentatively, as though she thought it might like to sniff her. Ms. Bosh was peering into a jar full of moths, and Mr. Hopper was making hoo-hoo-hoo noises at one of the owls, who did not look impressed.

Tap-tap-tap. It was coming from one of the windows. Olivia stared out into the darkness beyond the glass. It was hard to see anything—the sky was nearly moonless and the window faced the back of the house where there were no streetlights. She walked closer to get a better look. Out of the darkness the sole of a shoe abruptly appeared on the other side of the window and made three impatient taps against the glass. It startled Olivia so much that she jumped back and stood stock-still for a few seconds, her heart thumping hard in her chest. Cautiously, she approached the window again. Now she could just make out a shadowy shape that looked as though it were perched in midair.

"Come on, open the window," a muffled voice said from the other side of the glass. Olivia pushed up the window, letting in a burst of cold air that made her shiver. Just outside the window was one of the brownstone's little balconies, on the edge of which, facing her, sat a pretty girl with glossy black hair crisply cut just below her ears. She wore a long white nightgown and thin black boots, one of which was poised to tap again on the window. She pulled back her leg and smiled at Olivia, then pushed out her bottom lip and blew upward to move her thick bangs out of her eyes.

"What are you doing out there?" Olivia asked.

The girl shrugged. "Nothing much." She brought her hand to her lips, and Olivia could see that she was smoking a cigarette.

"Are you a student from Ms. Bender's?" Olivia asked.

"That's none of your business," the girl said. Then she added, "You're not going to call Ms. Bender and tell on me, are you?"

"No. How'd you get up here?" Olivia asked.

"Climbed." The girl blew a thin stream of smoke out of her mouth, and Olivia could taste it in the air.

"You shouldn't smoke, you know," Olivia said.

"There are a lot of things I shouldn't do." She smiled again at Olivia–a sort of lopsided smile. "I do them anyway." She took another drag on her cigarette and stared at Olivia with dark, penetrating eyes. "We should be friends, you and I," she said finally. "We have a lot in common."

"But you don't even know me," Olivia protested.

"I can tell plenty just by looking at you. You're a loner, same as me. And we're both smarter and more mature than most other kids, which is why we don't have friends–they're jealous of us. But you and I . . . we're equally matched. Put us together and hah! We'd give people a run for their money!" The girl smiled, showing a set of pretty white teeth.

Olivia guessed there was some truth in what she said. Olivia was a loner–sort of. And oftentimes she *did* suspect that she was smarter and more mature than most other kids her age. But still, she didn't like this girl. And she most definitely did not want to be friends with her.

"You better get back to Ms. Bender's before you get in trouble," Olivia said.

The girl stopped smiling. She looked offended, realizing that Olivia had rejected her offer of friendship. But then her expression grew cool again, and she took a final drag on her cigarette and flicked it off the balcony.

"Sure." She shrugged and stood up. "I was getting bored talking to you anyway. Just give me a hand, will you?"

"To do what?" Olivia asked.

"Getting down is harder than climbing up, you know. Just stand on the balcony and hold my hands while I try to get my footing on the top of the window casement below. I can jump down from there."

Olivia shook her head. "That's too far to jump. Better just come in through the window and walk downstairs."

"Oh sure! And get in trouble for trespassing? No, thank you. Just forget it. Don't help me. I'll manage on my own, just like I always do." The girl stood up to go.

"Fine," Olivia sighed. "I'll help you. Just hang on a sec." She lifted her leg and hooked it over the windowsill. But just as she was about to lift her other leg and hop down onto the balcony, she remembered something. This was the *back* of the brownstone. There *were* no balconies on the back of the brownstone, only on the front, facing the street.

Olivia looked at the girl, who was biting her lip, as if in anticipation of Olivia's next movement.

"You're a spirit, aren't you?" Olivia said.

The girl smirked, then her arm shot forward and grabbed Olivia's leg, which was still hanging over the sill. The girl's grip was powerful as she tugged at Olivia, trying to pull her outside, her sharp nails cruelly biting into Olivia's calf. Olivia put a hand on either side of the wall beside the window for leverage and pulled back with all her strength. The girl pulled harder, increasingly harder, while

Olivia resisted mightily, feeling all the while like she was being ripped in two. But the girl was too strong for her—Olivia was slowly but surely being pulled out the window, below which was nothing but a long, sheer drop to the pavement. A sudden, especially vicious yank made Olivia scream out in pain. The girl laughed, and in that second her grip loosened just the smallest bit, just enough for Olivia to manage a sharp, hard kick at the girl's face. The girl let out a piercing shriek and released Olivia's leg, which Olivia swiftly pulled back inside the room. She slammed the window shut and leapt back, afraid that the girl would come crashing through the glass.

Olivia waited and listened. Her legs were trembling, and she was breathing so hard, she was practically panting. After a while, when nothing happened, she slowly walked toward the window. She squinted and walked closer. The girl was gone. Olivia pressed her nose to the window. The balcony was gone too.

"Holy cow," Olivia whispered.

"There you are!" Ansel burst into the room, looking panicked and as though he had been running. "We were all getting worried. Ms. Bosh wondered if one of the birds had attacked you."

For the first time Olivia looked around and realized that there was no one else in the room with her.

"Where did everyone go?" Olivia asked dazedly.

"They all picked their harbingers twenty minutes ago. They said they left you gazing out the window, and assumed you were trying to decide which harbinger to tag. Are you all right, Olivia? You look rather shook up." Ansel gazed down at her anxiously.

"I can't have been here that long," Olivia muttered, looking at the window. "I spoke to her for only five minutes . . ."

"Spoke to whom?" Ansel put his hand beneath Olivia's chin and tipped it up so that her eyes met his, his face now very serious.

"The girl. She was a spirit. We fought . . ."

Ansel's blue eyes looked sharply into hers. "White dress? Short black hair?"

Olivia nodded.

"I'm afraid you just met Abby." Ansel shook his head angrily. "She's a nasty piece of work! My mother's been trying to get rid of her for years–it's very difficult to get rid of spirits at an Exit Academy. You had a tussle with her, you say?"

"She tried to pull me out the window," Olivia replied.

Since she had escaped from Abby's grip, she had not felt any pain, but now it bloomed again on her calf, where Abby had dug her nails in.

"And apparently she failed," Ansel exclaimed in wonder. "There's not many who could survive a scrap with Abby—man, woman, or child. Are you all right? Do you want to stop training for the evening?"

"Will she come back for me again?"

"It's possible, Olivia," Ansel admitted. "I'll keep a closer eye on you from here on in, but Abby is a clever girl."

Olivia's legs were still trembling and the pain in her calf was searing. There was nothing she would have liked better than to leave right then, to go back to bed and pull the covers up over her nose. But she thought of Nora's script. It was somewhere close by.

"I'm fine," she told Ansel. "I want to keep going."

Ansel studied her for a moment, then said, "My mother told me you were a most unusual child. All right. If you want to keep going, I suppose I can't stop you. Now we'd best get back before poor Ms. Bosh imagines we've *both* been pecked into tiny little pieces!"

TWENTY

The rest of the group was standing outside Room 42, and they were all visibly relieved when they saw Olivia coming up the hallway with Ansel.

"She's fine, she's fine," Ansel assured them to ward off their questions. "She just had trouble deciding on her harbinger."

"So what's next?" Ms. Krickle asked fretfully. "What will we have to do in this room?"

"Absolutely nothing," Ansel said, smiling at them. "I thought we all deserved to take a little break." He opened the door to a very cozy-looking diner. The walls were lined with little booths, and the tables had plates of sandwiches on them. There was a jukebox in the corner, and Elvis Presley's "Blue Suede Shoes" was playing.

"Now we're talking!" Mr. Hopper said, plopping down in a booth and picking up a sandwich. Ms. Bosh and Ms.

Krickle joined him, but Olivia took a booth by herself. She didn't want to take a break. She wanted to get this thing over with—find Nora's script and deliver it to Madame Brenda.

Ansel went behind the diner's counter, reached into a refrigerator, and gathered up a handful of little soda bottles.

"Who's thirsty?" he asked, and he handed each person a bottle of soda.

Ms. Bosh opened hers and took a swig, then immediately spit it out.

"Echhh! What is that stuff?" she cried.

"Spit-ade," Ansel responded. The spit-out beverage began to give off a pale nimbus of light, which grew stronger and began to stretch upward. It shifted, and knobs and lumps punched out of it here and there, so that it looked like a sack with a person inside who was trying to get out. Everyone watched, speechless. Olivia, however, had once seen something similar—when the ghost of Branwell had appeared in front of her.

"It's a spirit," Olivia whispered.

"Yes, it is," Ansel whispered back.

"You mean I spit a spirit out of my mouth?" Ms. Bosh asked.

"Spit a spirit, spit a spirit, sprit and siplet . . . ," Mr. Hopper said. "Say that three times fast, I dare any of you."

But no one took the dare. They were all watching as the spirit began to assume a more definite form. It now had legs and arms and was shaping up to be a portly fellow. His face emerged last, and it was a full, round face with thick eyebrows, a wide nose, thin lips, and a very amused-looking pair of eyes.

"Meet your guide," Ansel said to Ms. Bosh. "Each of you will have one." Then to the spirit he said, "Dave, isn't it?"

"In the flesh." Except he wasn't made of flesh exactly. He reminded Olivia of the cowgirl night-light she used to have when she was little. The cowgirl's skin was lighted from within by a tiny lightbulb. Dave also looked as though he had a lightbulb in the middle of his body.

Dave stepped forward and smiled at Ms. Bosh. "I love your hat," he said to her.

"You do?" Ms. Bosh said, clearly delighted. "*They* don't," she added accusingly.

"Oh, but it's very becoming," Dave said. "Not many could carry it off. Come." He held out his elbow and she hooked her arm in his. "Let's have a chat and get to know each other." He escorted her very tenderly to a corner booth.

"Who's the next to spit?" Ansel said.

Mr. Hopper stood up and opened his bottle, lifted it heartily in the air, and said, "Cheers!" Then he took a swig and spit it halfway across the room. Again, the Spit-ade began to emit a light, then a form, until a short, stout woman appeared in front of them. She marched up to Mr. Hopper and held out her hand.

"Name's Penny. Now, I'm not going to give you the soft sell, bub. The fact is you've spent the last fifty-seven years as a lazy good-for-nothing, whose idea of being productive is tearing open a fresh bag of corn chips. That's all going to change, pal. I'm going to whip you back into shape, and it's not going to be pretty, but you'll thank me by the end of it. Okay . . . move it." She gave Mr. Hopper a slap on his behind. "Let's go over the game plan."

Mr. Hopper looked at Ansel with a pained expression. "Can I change guides?"

"Afraid not." Ansel smiled, and he shrugged as Penny dragged Mr. Hopper to a booth.

"Next?" Ansel looked at Ms. Krickle and Olivia. When Olivia didn't say anything, Ms. Krickle sighed. "Okay, I'll go." She opened the bottle and sniffed it. "I don't smell anything." Then she took a drink and spit it out with much sputtering and grimacing.

She took a napkin from the booth and swabbed her

tongue with it so methodically that she missed the formation of her guide. Which was too bad, because it was spectacular. There were bursts of tiny fireworks within the column of light, and five hands popped out from the place where the head should have been, and the head emerged somewhere around the hip area, and it took a few seconds of hasty rearranging to get all the bits and pieces right. Finally, the guide appeared as a young man with a thick mop of long unruly hair, a snub nose, and long, loose, gangly limbs.

"Man, that was hard! I didn't think I'd make it through. I still think I might have put my left foot where the right one should be. And vice versa." He sat down on the floor and took off his shoes and socks. "Yeah, yeah, I did. See?" He held up one long skinny foot toward Ms. Krickle, who withdrew in disgust. Olivia could see that indeed his big toes were in the spot where the pinky toes should have been.

"And *this* is supposed to be my guide?" Ms. Krickle asked with disbelief.

"Ms. Krickle, meet Leon," Ansel said. Leon, still on the floor, waved at Ms. Krickle happily.

"Please put your socks and shoes back on," Ms. Krickle said stiffly. And then to Ansel, "He barely seems qualified to serve me a burger and fries, much less be my guide!"

"Each person's guide is tailored to suit the person per-

Cola
Cola
10¢

fectly," Ansel said. "You'll just have to trust the process, Ms. Krickle."

Leon jumped to his feet, leaving his shoes and socks in a pile. He stretched out in the booth, opposite Ms. Krickle, his bare feet crossed one over the other on the seat.

"So . . . what do you do for fun on a Saturday night?" Leon asked Ms. Krickle.

Ansel approached Olivia's booth and sat down. "Last but not least," he said.

Olivia hesitated. What if she spit the stuff out and nothing happened? After all, she wasn't *really* going to die. If no spirit guide emerged out of her spit, wouldn't Ansel get suspicious?

"Forget it," Olivia said, shaking her head.

"Nothing to be afraid of, my dear."

"I'm not afraid." She discreetly slipped the little bottle in the long side pocket of her jeans. "It's just that I refuse to drink stuff that tastes so nasty, people have to spit it out."

"You won't actually swallow it, Olivia."

"And what if I do?"

"You physically can't. It's so repulsive that you'll naturally spit it out."

"Then why would I want to put it in my mouth in the

first place? Anyway," Olivia crossed her arms over her chest, "I lost my bottle."

"That's okay." Ansel rose, fetched another bottle from the fridge, opened it, and put it down in front of her. "It doesn't have to be a specific bottle, you see–it's just that the liquid has to pick up some skin cells from your mouth, which automatically connects you with the right guide."

"I won't do it," Olivia said simply. Ansel rolled his eyes upward, as though silently asking for help, then rubbed his hand across his forehead in consternation.

"Look, Olivia, you have to connect with your guide before we can give you your script and pass you over. It's just the way things are done."

"You mean I can't get my script if I don't do this?" Olivia asked.

"Dreadfully sorry, but no, no you can't."

Olivia looked at the bottle of clear liquid apprehensively. She picked it up and sniffed at it. It had no odor. She put it to her lips and tipped out the tiniest bit into her mouth. In all her life she had never tasted anything so foul–a mixture of sour milk and burnt rubber–and she spit it out so forcefully that it shot clear across to the center of the room. The light began to glow off of the liquid and a figure rose out of it, forming itself quickly and efficiently. The spirit was a thin and lithe man, who at first glance looked young. He gazed around for a second, as though trying to get his bearings.

"Welcome." Ansel went up to him. "I don't think we've met before. Your name is?"

The spirit said nothing, just gazed at Ansel with his pale blue eyes, which were long and angled up like a cat's. Then he pointed a finger at Olivia and looked questioningly at Ansel.

"Yes," Ansel said. "She's yours."

There was something about that phrase that made Olivia feel chilled to the marrow. She watched as the spirit came toward her. He moved very quickly, so fast in fact that Olivia didn't even see his feet move, as though he had glided over to her. He stood in front of her, staring down. Up close his face was not young, but neither was it old. Instead it was the face of a person who had seen many things, like the faces from photographs in Olivia's world history textbook of soldiers coming home after a war. He had wide lips that seemed about to stretch into some definite expression—either a smile or a scowl—but that had stopped short and hovered somewhere between the two.

"Please, sit," Ansel told the spirit genially. "I'll leave you two alone and you can get acquainted."

Olivia sorely wanted to cry out, "No! Don't leave!" But she held her tongue as the spirit took a seat across from her.

Was this *really* her guide? she wondered. He didn't look like the others. He was more imposing somehow. And he gave her the heebie-jeebies. She remembered what Madame Brenda had told her, and a terrifying thought occurred to her: What if this was Abby, disguised as her guide?! Ansel had said she was clever.

Olivia removed her arms from the table and leaned back in her seat to keep her body as far away from the guide as possible. She kept her eyes fixed on the spirit, ready to spring away if it tried to grab her. She could hear all the others talking to their guides—easy, light conversations. But this spirit remained perfectly silent. The silence went on for so long that Olivia grew uncomfortable, then annoyed.

"Aren't you going to say something?" she snapped.

The spirit pointed at the table and Olivia looked down. In front of her was a folded piece of paper. It hadn't been there before, she was sure of it. She picked it up and unfolded it very slowly, as if something might pop out of it.

It was a child's drawing of a large house perched on top of a sheer, dangerous-looking cliff. Way below at the base of the cliff was the ocean, with large scalloped waves drawn in with a dark blue crayon, and a boat sitting up high on one of those waves, looking like it was caught in the middle of a hurricane. Olivia looked up at the spirit and frowned.

"This is *my* drawing," Olivia said. She had drawn it for her father when she was a little kid. He had put it up on the refrigerator in every apartment they'd lived in, until it finally got lost in one of the moves. "Where did you get this?" she demanded of the spirit.

He slid out of the booth and stood up, then bowed his head slightly as if saying good-bye.

"Wait a minute!" Olivia grabbed at him without thinking. Her hand touched his arm for a brief moment. It felt as though she were dipping her hand into ice water, and she quickly pulled it back and looked at it. The tips of her fingers on her right hand, where she had touched the spirit, were a horrible dead-white color, and she couldn't feel them at all. She looked up at the spirit, but he had gone.

She blew on her fingers to warm them, then tucked her hand beneath her arm. The numbness began to melt into a painful prickly feeling, which was almost worse than the numbness. Gradually, however, her fingers began to feel normal again, and she picked up the drawing. How peculiar! It was dog-eared and the paper had yellowed a bit, but it was her drawing, she was sure of it. She refolded it carefully and put it in her back pocket.

"Now that we've all met," Ansel announced to the room, "let us bid each other a temporary adieu. The orientation must continue, and you will have decades ahead of you to chat with your guides."

The guides stood up. Mr. Hopper's guide punched him on his shoulder by way of a good-bye, while Ms. Bosh's guide gave her a warm hug, and Ms. Krickle's guide gave her a big sloppy kiss on her cheek, which she didn't wipe off. Then the guides folded up like Chinese lanterns and were gone.

TWENTY-ONE

"If you'll all kindly follow me," Ansel said, "I'll show you to the Script Vault."

This is it, Olivia thought.

They stopped by a metal door, which looked something like the sort of giant safe you'd see in a bank, with a large combination lock in the middle of it. Ansel knelt by the door and began to turn the lock this way and that until finally there was a soft click, and he pulled the vault door open. Everyone except Olivia had to duck their heads in order not to hit them against the top of the vault's door. A low murmur erupted from the group as they looked around. Every wall from floor to ceiling was filled with bookshelves squeezed tight with manuscripts. There had to be thousands upon thousands of them! Several ladders with wheels on the bottom stretched from the floor to the ceiling, where they were attached to a bar.

"The scripts are alphabetized by last name, so you should have no trouble finding your own," Ansel said. "I'll give you a few minutes to scout them out. We'll be rehearsing these scripts later, and in the end we will present a complete performance, with props and scenery and music."

As soon as Ansel left, closing the vault door behind him, everyone rushed to the shelves and began searching for their names.

Okay, Olivia thought. Nora Horn. She walked along the shelves until she found the *H*s printed on the manuscripts' spines. Mr. Hopper was already on the ladder standing just above her. "H-o, H-o-n," Mr. Hopper said, searching through the shelves. "H-o-o. H-o-p . . . here I am!" Olivia looked up at Mr. Hopper as he took the manuscript off the bookshelf. On the cover it said *A Twist of Fate.*

Mr. Hopper quickly leafed through his script. "It says in mine that I'm going to choke on a pretzel," he said. "Well, that seems kind of harsh." And after considering for a moment, he asked, "I wonder if I'll get to rehearse with *actual* pretzels."

Standing high up on another ladder, Ms. Krickle snorted.

"What?!" Mr. Hopper cried. "It's a legitimate question."

Olivia continued to scour the shelf for Nora's script. There were several *Horns*, but no *Nora Horns*. She checked again and again, in case she had missed it, and then she checked all the manuscripts on either side of the *Horns*, but she found no *Noras*.

Maybe Madame Brenda had been mistaken. Perhaps the script was somewhere else altogether. Or it might simply have been accidentally misplaced in the vault. Olivia looked around the room. All the scripts were neat and straight and looked as if they had been shelved by an extraordinarily meticulous librarian. No, it seemed unlikely that a script would be misplaced here. But, Olivia considered, Ansel might have deliberately *hidden* it in the wrong place.

Olivia looked around the room gloomily. It would take her hours to check all the shelves. Olivia leaned her forehead against the scripts and closed her eyes, trying hard to think, despite the exclamation from Ms. Krickle, "Found it!" and then Ms. Bosh's "Oh, here's mine!"

Suddenly Olivia remembered something Frannie had told her. That when she had been banned from checking out *Romeo and Juliet*, she had hidden the book behind some other books. Olivia took a deep breath, then began to walk around the room. She did it methodically, starting with the books on the lower shelves, her eyes scanning them quickly as she went. Ms. Bosh, Ms. Krickle, and Mr. Hopper were already sitting at a table in the center of the room, studying their scripts, but they looked up now.

"What's wrong?" Mr. Hopper asked. "Can't find your script?" But Olivia didn't bother to answer–there was no time.

She completed the first round, then stepped on a ladder and started to look a few shelves higher, grabbing on to the edge of the shelves and pushing off to the side to move the ladder along the wall. As her eyes grew accustomed to skimming the spines, she moved faster and faster, the ladder clattering on the floor and turning sharply at the corners of the wall. Ansel would be back any minute. Olivia's heart was racing and her arms ached from pushing the ladder around, but she kept at it, much to the chagrin of the other three.

"Children should be supervised," Ms. Krickle complained, looking up from her script. "This is not a playground."

Olivia was nearly at the end of the second round when she saw something unusual: the *Taubman, Darlene* and *Taubman, Darren* scripts were pushed out a little farther than the others. Just a little bit, but it was enough. Olivia tipped the scripts out and sure enough, shoved behind them was another script. She reached back and pulled the hidden script out. On its cover was the title *Flirting With Death.* She turned it over and checked its spine—*Horn, Nora.* Olivia smiled and silently thanked Frannie just as she heard the sound of the vault's combination lock clicking. Olivia quickly turned Nora's script so that the title faced her chest. Ansel strolled in and looked around at them all.

"Everyone found their script? All right then, onward and upward. At least we hope it's upward, don't we?" He winked.

They filed out of the vault, and as they started back down the hallway, Ansel said, "We'll find some open studios and start rehearsals pronto, as some of you will be departing soon." The hallway began to wind around on itself tightly here, and there were many doors on this part of the floor, which Ansel kept opening, checking for empty rooms. After opening one of the doors, he turned to the others and gestured for them to come closer.

"This is the final dress rehearsal for one of our students," Ansel whispered. "He'll be performing later this evening. You might want to have a peek—he's quite good."

They all gathered around and peered into the room through the partly open door. Inside were two scaffolds hung by wires from the ceiling in front of two sheets of glass, also hung by wires. Two men, one on each scaffold, stood with their backs to the audience. They were each holding a squeegee and had a bucket of soapy water on their scaffolds.

"Oooh, I get it–they're window washers," Ms. Bosh whispered.

"Hey, pal, you ought to see what I'm seeing," said the man on the right-hand scaffold as he wiped at the window with his rag.

"Yeah?" the other man said. "Whataya seeing?"

"A good-lookin' receptionist."

"Ahh, you got all the luck. All I'm seeing is a bald guy in a suit picking his teeth with a paper clip. I ain't got no luck, I tell you."

Olivia realized that the man on the left-hand scaffold was none other than Louie.

"Hey, step on over here and take a gander," the other man offered.

"Yeah? Hey, that's real decent of you. Thanks." As Louie took a step toward the other man, he tipped over his bucket of soapy water, skidded off the edge of the scaffold, and fell, hitting a stack of padded cushions on the floor below.

"Oooh," they all said in unison.

"He really does have extraordinarily bad luck," Ansel said, shutting the door.

When they continued on, Olivia lagged behind until, as the others went around a corner, she suddenly turned and bolted in the other direction, running so fast that she nearly knocked over an old man, then managed to just miss tripping over the legs of someone emerging from the OUT chute, until she finally reached the door to the stairs. She flung it open so hard that it slammed shut with a bang, and she started a mad dash up the circular stairs. She looked behind her once, just to make sure Ansel hadn't followed her, and it was then that her foot skidded off the edge of the step. She stumbled, and she instinctively put out her hands to stop herself. The next second she heard the ruffling of paper and a soft splash. She cried out, "No!" but even as she said it, she could see the script in the water below, caught in a whirling eddy at the base of the stairs. The pages splayed out and began to spin, and then Nora's script was swiftly carried off by the current and disappeared.

Just then the third-floor door whipped open and Nora, dressed in pajamas, was looking down at Olivia, who was on her hands and knees on the steps. Nora narrowed her eyes and shook her head.

"What are we going to do with you, kid? Huh?" Then,

to Olivia's surprise she knelt down, draped one of Olivia's arms over her shoulder, and lifted her across her back like a sack of chicken feed.

"Let me down, Nora, please!" Olivia cried. "I've dropped something! I've got to try to get it back! It's *very* important!"

But Nora ignored her completely, keeping a firm hold of Olivia even as she struggled to break free. She carried her up to Olivia's bedroom, kicked the door closed, and deposited Olivia on the bed.

"So. You're hitting the booze again, huh?" Nora said. She sat down on the bed, and when Olivia tried to get up, Nora pinned her arms down firmly.

"Nora, please! Let me go!" Olivia imagined the script getting flung about, torn apart, destroyed. Her panic was escalating, and she struggled like a wild cat against Nora's grip, but to no avail.

"You are out of control, kid!" Nora shouted at Olivia. "Falling down drunk in the middle of the night–"

"Nora," Olivia said, wiggling her wrists to try to free them from Nora's grip, "I DO NOT DRINK!"

"No? Then what's this poking out of your pocket?" She let go of Olivia's right arm and swiftly reached into Olivia's side pocket to pull out the little bottle of Spit-ade.

"That's not alcohol," Olivia said.

"Really, kid, I wasn't born yesterday," Nora said. She let go of Olivia, unscrewed the Spit-ade's cap, and took a sniff. She frowned and sniffed it again. Then she took a quick swig and spit it out, gagging.

Olivia sat up and watched. The spill began to glow and the glow began to stretch. She looked over at Nora. She had stopped gagging and was watching the light too. It was a slow, careful light that formed itself as it rose. Feet, legs, arms–it was dressed in shorts and a sleeveless red T-shirt–shoulders, neck, so that even before his face was formed, Olivia knew who it was. She smiled. "Hi, Christopher," she said. "This is Nora."

TWENTY-TWO

"I know. We've already met," Christopher said.

Nora looked at him with some confusion. After a moment, she nodded. "Yeah, I think we *have* met."

"Do you remember where?" Christopher asked. Nora considered this for a moment.

"Here. I think it was here, wasn't it?" Nora asked.

Christopher nodded. "I came here for classes at the same time as you. I remember when you first walked in. You were dressed in a hospital gown and your hair was all wild, and you said to Ansel, 'Okay, buster, how about you give me the crash course. I don't like to waste time.' Do you remember what he said?"

Nora shook her head at first, but then she answered slowly, "He said I'd already given *myself* the crash course on my motorcycle."

"That's exactly what he said. I think you laughed."

"I think I did."

"Does this mean you're Nora's guide?" Olivia asked.

"I will be, when she needs one. But she doesn't need me yet."

"But Christopher, she has a script. It was there, in the vault. I had it, I had it and it fell into the water," Olivia said.

"It doesn't matter," Christopher said.

"But it does!" Olivia insisted. "She needs it to cross. She needs to know how it happens."

"She does know how it happens. So do I. We rehearsed it together, over and over again."

"I don't remember . . . ," Nora said, a look of hopelessness crossing her face.

"I played Ansel's role," Christopher said. "Because Ansel thought it would be funny if he was the one who played Madame Brenda. And who was it that played Olivia?"

Nora shook her head. "I don't know . . . I don't remember . . ." She frowned suddenly and after a pause said, "Wait. I think her name was Mrs. Fleishman."

"That's right!" Christopher said. "Mrs. Fleishman wasn't very good, but when she dropped the script into the water, she made the funniest little squeak."

"I don't get it," Olivia said.

Christopher turned to Nora. "Do you want to do the final scene?"

"I don't know if I can," Nora hedged.

"Come on," Christopher said. "I'm pretty rusty too. I'll start, okay?" Christopher leapt up on Olivia's bed and lay back, his legs crossed. He composed his features so that they looked lazy and sort of pouty. "Nora, dear, what do you say to a game of gin rummy? I'm feeling lucky this morning."

Olivia giggled. It was a perfect imitation of Ansel.

Nora hesitated. Then she sat down on the bed and started to say, "Not–"

"Wait," Christopher said. "Aren't you supposed to be rowing?"

"Right," Nora said. She got up on her knees and pretended to be rowing. "Not this morning, Ansel. I'm not really in the mood for cards."

"Checkers, then?" Christopher said.

"No," Nora said. "I–I–Oh man, I can't do this, Christopher."

Christopher sat up. "You can, Nora. You're ready," he said, as himself and not as Ansel.

"But you don't understand. It's still painful when I go

outside. I feel like I can't breathe. I feel like I'm being crushed."

Then Olivia remembered something: "Your toe moved. Yesterday, while you were outside on the skateboard, your toe moved in the hospital."

"You see," Christopher said. "That means you were waking up. You were coming back to life! That's wonderful, Nora! And of course it hurt. You were feeling your body—the body that's lying in the hospital bed, badly injured. Come on, Nora, you can do this. Let's try again." Christopher lay back down on the bed and made his expression into Ansel's. "Checkers, then?"

Nora took a breath. Started to row. "No. I'm not in the mood for games. Actually, Ansel, I wanted to tell you something."

"Make it something perfectly delightful."

"It's not. It's something perfectly horrible," Nora said.

"Then don't tell me, please. You can tell it to my mother. She loves horrible stories!"

"Ansel, my script was lost because I hid it."

"But Nora, darling, why would you?" Christopher asked.

"I didn't want to leave here. I wasn't ready. My body was in so much pain. But I felt okay here. There was no pain at all. And you became more my family than my real family ever was. It was just easier to forget everything, you know. To forget what the script said."

"What did it say?" Olivia couldn't stop herself from asking.

Nora stopped rowing and looked at her.

"Tell her," Christopher said.

"It said . . . it said that in the end, I would choose to live."

Christopher sat up and clapped, although his hands made no sound. "Bravo! You could be an actress, you know."

"I always kind of wanted to be," Nora admitted.

"But what happens at the end of the play?" Olivia asked.

"Oh, there's this whole big emotional scene," Christopher said. "And then the toilet starts running, so the boat gets thrown around and they lose an oar . . . hey, Nora, you want to do the end for Olivia?"

"All right. Where should we start?"

"How about after we get off the boat and we're standing in the front hallway?"

Nora stood up and went to Olivia's door. Christopher joined her and they looked at each other for a little while before Nora said, "I guess I should go, Ansel."

"Does it have to be now?" Christopher asked, as Ansel.

Nora shrugged. "It's not raining, snowing, or hailing, so I guess today is as good as any day." She hesitated, then threw her arms around Christopher, and he hugged her back tightly. They stayed that way for a minute while Olivia averted her eyes. Somehow it just seemed too personal to watch. Then Nora withdrew from Christopher and opened the door to leave.

"Wait," Christopher said. He offered her his arm, which Nora took. "I'll walk with you." And they walked out of the bedroom and shut the door behind them. The last words were Nora's, from behind the door: "So long, kid. Good luck with the ollie! And stay off the hooch!"

Olivia clapped, quietly so that she wouldn't wake her father. Then she got up and opened the door in time to see Nora heading down the stairs, but Christopher was gone altogether.

Olivia sat down on her bed, letting the events of the evening run through her mind, and it occurred to her that she had never really needed to steal the script in the first place. Sure, Nora might have forgotten what was in her script, but both Christopher and Ansel had rehearsed it many times—Christopher even knew it all by heart! She thought about Madame Brenda, and all the things she had told her: that

Olivia was a Straddler, and that she was the only person who could help Nora. That she was special. It was all just a big fat lie to get Olivia to go into the Exit Academy and play the role that was written in Nora's script—the role of a girl who finds the script, then stupidly drops it!

Madame Brenda was probably laughing at me the whole time, Olivia thought bitterly.

Her anger swelled until she couldn't stand it any longer. She stood up and marched straight downstairs to Madame Brenda's room. She knocked on the door loudly, and when she didn't immediately hear anything, she opened it and stepped inside. Madame Brenda was sitting in bed, reading a paperback book, on the cover of which was a handsome man dressed as a gladiator kissing a dark-haired woman in a toga. Madame Brenda quickly closed the book and put it under her pillow, then said, "The thing about knocking, darling, is that you must also give the person a chance to say, 'Come in.' " She lifted her reading glasses and examined Olivia. "Well, you don't look any worse for the wear."

"All the stuff you told me about being a Straddler was a lie, wasn't it?" Olivia blurted out furiously. "And the only reason you needed me especially was because my name was in the script, not because my 'spirit is built differently' and blah, blah, blah."

"Are you telling me I'm a liar, cupcake?" Madame Brenda asked. She stared hard at Olivia in a very formidable way. "Or are you *asking* me if you are indeed a Straddler?" She smiled and said, "Let's assume you're asking—it's much more pleasant that way. And here's your answer: Yes, darling, you are very much a Straddler. And it mattered extremely that it was *you* who fetched the script. You see, scripts are not written in stone. Yes, they are the most *likely* way that a person will die, but the script can change. For instance, someone may have a great change of heart, much like your friend Stacy. Or sometimes a spirit interferes, meddles in human affairs, and changes the outcome."

"But why did Nora even need a script in the first place, if she was going to choose to live?" Olivia objected.

"Nora's case was most unusual. Yes, she chose to live, but there was a great deal of risk written into Nora's script, because Nora is a young woman who loves taking risks—and our death scripts, you see, echo the way we live our lives. To send a Straddler into an Exit Academy is a very serious business. There are many things that could have gone horribly wrong. If you had not found the script, Nora would have drifted off and become a lost spirit. Or if, heaven forbid, something had happened to *you,* we would have lost both of you. But oh, Olivia, I had great faith in you, as did Ansel. And we were right! You've succeeded beautifully, cupcake!"

Olivia felt a rush of pride, then winced at the sudden ache from the bruises on her calf—a souvenir from Abby.

"Wait a minute," Olivia suddenly realized, feeling her anger rising again. "What about Ansel? He must have known why I was in the academy all along. Come to think of it, he must have known why my father and I were invited to come live here. And the whole time he was just pretending . . ."

"Of course. But, darling, don't you see, he *had* to let the thing play itself out. It's part of his job. And anyway, you can't possibly stay mad at him for too long . . . he's much too charming, and such a handsome face! Now," Madame Brenda stretched her arms out toward Olivia and wiggled her fingers, "give us a kiss good night and then off to bed."

After Olivia gave Madame Brenda a quick kiss on her cheek, Madame Brenda reached under the bed and pulled out Olivia's toolbox.

"Here you go, darling, safe and sound," Madame Brenda said. Then she retrieved her book from under her pillow and Olivia turned to leave.

"Olivia? . . ." Madame Brenda called as Olivia opened the door.

"Yes?"

"Promise me one thing?"

"Okay," Olivia said.

"Promise me you'll clean out your pores every night, darling. Really, they're a mess."

TWENTY-THREE

Olivia slept late the next day, even though the dazzling morning sun filtered through her curtains and flooded the whole room with its honey-colored light. She probably would have slept well into the afternoon if the knock on her door hadn't woken her.

"Come in," she called groggily.

The door opened and George Kidney walked in, carrying a breakfast tray loaded with a plate of pancakes, a bottle of syrup, and a tall glass of orange juice.

"It's not my birthday today, you know," Olivia said. He always brought her peanut butter–chocolate chip pancakes on the morning of her birthday.

"Can't I bring my daughter pancakes in bed if I feel like it?" George said. He was obviously in a very good mood.

"You can bring her pancakes in bed *every* morning if you feel like it," Olivia said, sitting up and throwing the covers off.

"Well," George said as he put the tray down over Olivia's legs, "actually I did have something to tell you." He sat down on the edge of the bed while Olivia poured syrup over her pancakes. "Ansel has fired me."

Olivia abruptly put down the syrup and stared at her father. "Oh, Dad, no," she said miserably.

"I thought you said you hated it here anyway," George said. He picked up her fork, cut off and speared a hefty piece of pancake, then held it out to her. She eyed it, knowing she should resist, that she should be mad at him. But it had loads of chocolate chips in it . . . She leaned forward and took a bite.

"Dad, you know I always hate places in the beginning," she objected with her mouth full.

"So you didn't really mind being here?" George asked.

"No."

"Good. Because although Ansel did fire me as his handyman, he hired me back as his cook."

"His cook! Really? No kidding?"

"No kidding. As long as I promised not to touch the plumbing ever again."

"That seems fair," Olivia said. She smiled. They were going to stay in one place for a while. That had never happened before. She suddenly wondered about Ruben—

whether he lived in the neighborhood. If maybe they would wind up in the same school.

"All right, Sweetpea, I'd better get down to the kitchen and start thinking about a lunch menu." George got up, then added, "It's not quite like being a cowboy, but it's a close second."

Olivia had nearly finished her pancakes when she remembered that today was the day she was meeting with Christopher. She dressed and headed downstairs, where she found that the water was still a little rough. In the distance, she could hear the toilet running, which meant it was only bound to get rougher. As she rowed through the canal, it struck her afresh that this was going to be her home, for a while at least. She wouldn't have to change schools every few months. She wouldn't have to memorize a new phone number. And maybe, sometime down the line, she could even have a slumber party.

She moored the boat in the lagoon and practically skipped out the door (but stopped herself before anyone could see, since skipping was a little ridiculous at twelve years old, even if it felt nice). Parked outside was a tremendously long black limousine, whose driver was leaning against the hood and staring up at the sky.

The top landing of the School for Superior Children was strewn with luggage, and Ms. Bender was standing in the midst of it, gesticulating angrily. "You! Boy!" she called down to the limousine driver. "Stop dawdling and carry this luggage to the car! You! I know you can hear me, you insipid lout, what!"

The driver didn't move a muscle, just kept staring up at the sky. Right then the school's front door opened and Stacy walked out, dressed in jeans and a T-shirt but looking somehow less sloppy than she did in her uniform.

"Good-bye, Ms. Bender," she said, without a whole lot of warmth, but Ms. Bender grabbed her and hugged her and kissed both her cheeks.

"I'm very proud of you," Ms. Bender said. "It was the hair color that won them over, of course."

"Sure, I guess," Stacy said doubtfully. She picked up a suitcase and started down the stairs. The driver instantly rushed over to help her.

"Thanks," Stacy said as he took the suitcase from her.

"And when you're done with that one, boy," Ms. Bender called, "you can come up here and fetch the rest."

"His name ain't Boy, it's Charlie!" Stacy snapped back at Ms. Bender, who, offended, turned and retreated inside.

When Stacy went back up the stairs to grab another bag, Olivia leaned over the railing. "So things went well with the Vondychomps, I guess?" she said. Stacy looked at her strangely, then nodded quickly and picked up another bag.

She acts like she doesn't recognize me, Olivia thought. Then she realized that she had spoken to Stacy while Stacy was dreaming–of course she wouldn't remember. But Stacy looked back at Olivia and said, "You're my sister's friend, ain't you? Don't go anywhere, she's got something for you." She opened the school's front door and yelled, "Hey, Frannie! That kid from next door is out here!"

In a minute Frannie came running out, carrying a large, flat object that looked like it had been hastily gift wrapped. "Oh, good," Frannie said when she saw Olivia. "I was scared I'd miss you! So . . . we're off. Mom and Claude are getting married next month."

"You fooled them then?" Olivia asked.

"Nah. Mr. Vondychomps's no dummy. I think he saw right through us. But my guess is he knows that Mom and Claude are a pretty good match anyway, and besides, I think he's kind of lonely in that big house, just him and Claude. Plus, he took a liking to me and Dij–I mean Stacy. She insists on being called by her real name now. Gets all uppity if you call her Dijon. Anyway, this is for you—to remember me by." Frannie handed Olivia the present over the brownstone banister. "Use both hands, it's heavy."

She wasn't exaggerating. It had to weigh about five pounds. Olivia sat down on the steps and unwrapped it while Frannie leaned across the banister and watched. Inside there was a flat rock with jagged edges.

"Turn it over," Frannie said. Olivia did and on the other side was a small painting of an animal, done in faded reds and browns.

"Is that an elephant?" Olivia asked.

"Nope, it's a mastodon," Frannie said. "Isn't it cool? It's the paperweight that Mr. Vondychomps gave me. He said his great-great-great-great—etcetera grandfather made it. It's part of a larger painting, I think. I know you're not supposed to give away a gift, but I wanted to give you something, and this was the nicest thing I had. I asked Mr. Vondychomps if he minded and he said that it was mine, so I could do whatever I wanted with it."

"Wow. Thanks." Olivia looked down at the painting. "Is the mastodon smiling?" she asked.

"Yeah. Isn't that weird?" Frannie said.

Olivia looked back down at the paperweight more closely. The mastodon was definitely smiling—a big, toothy, goofy smile. "No, that's not weird at all," she said, smiling herself. "Hey, hang on a sec."

Olivia ran back inside the house, opened the coat closet, and pulled out the Princepessa's wrap. Behind the double doors, she could hear the splash of an oar in the lagoon and voices muffled by rushing water. She rummaged through the hallway desk and found a pen and a scrap of paper, on which she scribbled:

Dear Mr. Vondychomps,

I'm pretty sure this once belonged to you. If so, meet me at five o'clock P.M. at the Babatavian Café, which is in the basement of the Here Hair shop on 71st Street and Broadway.

Yours truly,

Princepessa Christina Lilli

P.S. I'm a much nicer person now than I used to be, I promise!

Olivia ran back outside and handed the fur wrap and note to Frannie.

"Give these to Mr. Vondychomps, okay? It's important," Olivia said.

"Sure," Frannie said. The driver honked the horn, and Stacy, who was already sitting in the car, gestured to Frannie to get in. Frannie shrugged. "Well, I guess I'd better go." They paused for an awkward moment. "Hey, do you think, maybe, we could hang out sometime?"

"Sure," Olivia said, and then, partially to hear herself say it, she added, "you know where I live."

Frannie leaned over the railing and gave Olivia a quick, embarrassed hug, then ran down the stairs, clutching the wrap and the note, and scrambled into the limousine.

Olivia waited until they drove off, waving once, though she wasn't sure that Frannie was looking anymore. Then she looked up and down the block. When she saw there was no one there, she shut her eyes. She imagined Christopher's face, which was very easy to do since she had seen it so clearly the night before. She imagined him doing an imitation of Ansel, and laughed. Suddenly she felt a warmth in her belly and she knew he was there.

"Hi, Christopher," she said in her head.

"Some fun last night, huh, kiddo? It was a good break from old Barry McFarkle."

"Oh, I forgot about him. How's he doing?"

"There's been some progress. Yesterday he covered his entire face in lard and was about to deep-fry it, but right before he dipped his head in boiling oil, he stopped and said, 'You know what? This might really hurt.' "

"That's an improvement," Olivia said.

"I thought so too. But later on someone found him wedged down a chimney. Looks like we still have more work to do."

"Hey, Christopher, I was thinking about it and you lied to me," Olivia said. "When I first told you about Ansel, you said you didn't know anything about him."

"I was . . . yeah, I was lying. But look, Olivia, it's like when you were three and you were on that climbing ladder in the playground. I had to let you find your own way down."

"If I ask you another question, are you going to lie to me?" Olivia said.

"Depends," Christopher responded cagily. "Try me."

"Last night, when I drank the Spit-ade, I met my guide. At least, I think he was my guide. Do you know anything about him?"

Christopher hesitated. "I know who he is." His voice was serious. "And there are lots of rumors about him. But rumors hardly ever pan out as truth, kiddo."

"He gave me a drawing that I did when I was a little kid–a house on top of a high cliff, with water underneath. And a boat."

"I remember it. Dad always hung it on the refrigerator. Did he say why he gave it to you?" said Christopher.

"He didn't say anything. Not a word."

"Yeah, well, that doesn't surprise me. Look, Olivia, I'd hold on to that drawing. Put it away somewhere safe. There's a reason why he wanted you to have it. You'll just have to be patient and wait to find out what it is."

The brownstone door opened, and Olivia turned to see Nora and Ansel.

Nora shrugged and said to Ansel, "It's not raining, snowing, or hailing, so I guess today is as good as any day." She hesitated, then threw her arms around Ansel, and he hugged her back tightly. Then Nora withdrew and started down the stairs.

"Wait," Ansel said, and he offered her his arm. "I'll walk with you."

Arm in arm they descended the stairs. Nora reached down and ruffled Olivia's hair. "So long, kid," she said. "Good luck with the ollie! And stay off the hooch!"

Ansel looked at Olivia and smiled, then winked meaningfully.

In a flash of recognition Olivia said to Christopher, "This is it, isn't it?! This is the script."

But Christopher didn't answer. He was watching,

through Olivia's eyes, as Nora and Ansel walked down the street. Bit by bit, Nora began to blur around the edges, until she appeared to be a quirk of summer sunlight, playfully accompanying a handsome young man in a beige linen suit as he strolled down the street alone, and then, suddenly, she was gone.

"Oh, Christopher!" Olivia cried. "Has she died?"

"No, no, not at all. She's just returned to her body in the hospital."

"Will she be okay then?" Olivia asked anxiously.

"You know I can't predict the future, but if I had to take a mad stab at the truth, I'd say she'll be fine. It'll be a slow recovery, but Nora is a pretty tough customer. And what's this about an ollie, kiddo?"

"Oh. Right," Olivia said. "I meant to tell you. I gave Jezebel away. I just . . . I tried to learn how to skateboard, I really did, but I'm not all that coordinated, you know, and there's this guy who's really good, the way you used to be—"

"That's fine, kiddo, really. I understand. You did the right thing. So what's on the agenda for today?"

"I was thinking we could go down to Seventy-fourth Street," Olivia said, getting up.

"What's on Seventy-fourth Street?" Christopher asked.

"The Xerox shop where Bineta works."

"Bineta? That goddess from Senegal? She was something, wasn't she? Why do you want to go see Bineta?"

"I just thought you might want to see her again," Olivia replied. But then she admitted, "Plus, I think I may wind up being a tall girl, and I kind of want to watch the way she walks."

TURN THE PAGE
FOR THE NEXT ADVENTURE
FEATURING OLIVIA KIDNEY...

olivia kidney

AND THE SECRET BENEATH THE CITY

one

Olivia Kidney had never been much of a morning person. Nor was she the sort of person who rushed gleefully into new situations. In fact, early mornings and new situations always made her feel especially rotten, which is why she chose to take the 7th Avenue IRT subway on Wednesday morning, the first day at her new middle school. She might have taken the bus, but "bus people" tended to be chirpy, orange-lipsticked old ladies on their way to the senior center for a day of creaky aerobics and pasty grilled cheese. Or else they were noisy little kids comparing their brand-new backpacks and glow-in-the-dark pens. "Bus people" were the sort of people who thought that the day was going to be one big, worry-free party, complete with a piñata full of goodies to take home at the end. In other words, they were the sort of people who didn't have a clue.

"Subway people," on the other hand, all looked like they were on their way to have their wisdom teeth removed. Which was exactly how Olivia felt that morning.

All the seats on the train were taken, so she clung to a pole in the center, trying not to whack people with her backpack. It wasn't easy, since her backpack was stuffed so full that it looked like her spine was nine months pregnant. That in itself was just wrong, Olivia thought. *Regular* schools didn't make you carry that much junk on the first day of classes. All over the city, kids were carrying droopy, deflated backpacks, but because she was going to a *special* school, Olivia had to haul hers around like a pack mule.

Attending the Malcolm Flavius School for the Arts had not been her idea.

"The kids who go to that school are talented, Dad. *Really* talented," Olivia had objected when her dad insisted she try out for the art program months ago.

"You're talented, Sweetpea," her dad had replied. "You have what they call *raw talent.* All it needs is a little seasoning."

George Kidney talked in food terms a lot these days. Until recently he had been a handyman–an appallingly bad handyman. But now he was personal chef to Ansel Plover, the owner of the brownstone they lived in.

"Dad, I couldn't get into that school if I was smothered in barbecue sauce."

And she was right. She took their art test, and they turned her down flat. But she didn't care. In fact, for the first time in many years, Olivia was looking forward to going to the regular local school, since she would actually know someone there. For most of her life, she'd been forced to switch schools so many times that she never had a chance to make any real friends. Now she had one: Ruben, a whiz of a skateboarder and a pretty decent guy too. She had met him over the summer, and now he was teaching her how to skateboard in Central Park—without too much success, but never mind—and they'd both been excited about going to the same school, a fact that neither one would be caught dead admitting.

"So that means I'm going to have to put up with your lousy mood swings in school too?" Ruben had said when they'd found out they were both zoned for Middle School 72.

"Don't worry," Olivia assured him. "If we run into each other in the hallway, I'll be sure to completely ignore you." But after they had parted that day, Olivia had walked home trying so hard to suppress her smiles that she had to clap her hand over her mouth a couple of times.

Then, a month ago, she had received a letter from the Malcolm Flavius School for the Arts saying that a spot had opened up and she would be admitted after all. For a solid week she argued about it with her father, but in the end she finally agreed to go, on the condition that if she hated it, she could switch to Middle School 72. And she was 100 percent sure that she would hate it.

The subway lurched to a halt. Olivia whipped around to check the station, walloping the man standing behind her with her backpack. Inside it were the requisite art supplies: charcoal sticks; a large tin of colored pencils; some square packages of blue erasers that you could squish but made your fingers smell bad; a box of pastels; a set of various pencils that looked like normal pencils but that the salesman at the art store assured her, with a smirk, were not; a pad of something called newsprint, which felt like the paper towels in public bathrooms, and a regular sketchpad, both of which were too large for her backpack and poked out of the top.

"Sorry," Olivia said to the man she'd walloped.

"Yep," he said gruffly, as though that was exactly the sort of thing he'd expected to happen that morning.

Seventy-second Street. The school was on 65th Street and West End Avenue. Only one more stop to go. Olivia checked her watch. She was early. Good. It would give her a chance to talk with her older brother, Christopher, before school.

A new rush of people shuffled into the car and Olivia turned to back up, smacking the same man with her backpack again.

"Hey, Santa Claus," he snarled, "if you hit me with your sack of crap one more time, I'm going to boot you straight back to the North Pole."

"Sorry," Olivia said. She slipped the backpack off her shoulders and carried it in her arms, just to be safe.

The train started up again, and Olivia stared out the window, pretending to be fascinated by the passing metal beams in the tunnel. In truth, though, she was looking for ghosts. It was a habit, a thing she'd done ever since she was seven and a little girl who lived next door told her there were ghosts in the subways.

"You can see them if you look out the window while you're in the tunnels," the girl had told Olivia. "They're little kids. They'll stick their tongues out at you when they float by. Their tongues are black, by the way."

"I don't believe in ghosts," Olivia had told the girl. And she didn't when she was seven. Since then, she had discovered that ghosts did indeed exist, but she'd never seen one with a black tongue, and besides, the little girl who told her about them was a chronic liar.

Still, you never know, Olivia reasoned as she gazed out the window into the murky tunnel. The world is a strange place.

The train slowed, then stopped at the 66th Street station, where Olivia squeezed her way out of the car, taking care to avoid the man whom she'd thwacked with her backpack.

She walked down Broadway to West End Avenue, catching sight of the school before she was even halfway down the block. Considering that it was a school for the arts, it was unbelievably ugly. Constructed as a large and perfectly square chunk of gray-tinted glass, it looked exactly like a gigantic television set. In fact, through the glass you could make out shadowy figures walking around, as though it were tuned to some weird sci-fi channel.

As Olivia approached, she examined the kids milling around on the street outside. They were all artists of some kind or other—dancers, singers, painters, musicians. Quite a few of them seemed eager to let everyone know exactly what sort of art they practiced, like the two whippet-thin girls who were dressed in leotards, short skirts, and tights, their hair yanked back into skull-pinching buns. And just in case there was any doubt, they each had a pair of ballet slippers conspicuously slung over their shoulders and one of them carried a pink canvas bag that said, "Dance Diva!"

Olivia rolled her eyes.

There were many kids carrying instrument cases, but for the most part they didn't seem show-offy. In fact, a couple of them looked as nervous as she felt, although she was certain that they didn't have half as much reason to be. At least they had some kind of a talent.

She scanned the area for a quiet place in which she could have a quick chat with Christopher. When he was alive, Christopher was the person Olivia would go to whenever she was worried about something. Now that he was dead, he was a little busier than he had been, but Olivia could still get a hold of him in a pinch. And she was feeling pretty pinched at the moment.

She walked around the perimeter of the school and found a narrow alcove sliced into the side of the building and a short flight of stairs that led up to a green metal door, which looked like it might be a service entrance. Olivia sat on the steps. She took a deep breath and began to think about Christopher: his smooth blond hair, the square-ish snub to his nose, his voice, which was slow paced and always sounded like he was talking to you while lying out in the sun. Olivia's breath grew deeper and she could smell his skin, salty, with that boy smell of sweat and a T-shirt that needed washing—well, it was the truth, that *was* how he smelled when he was alive. Gradually she began to feel a melting warmth in her stomach, and she knew he was coming through. It took longer than usual, and as she waited, she pretended to be tying her shoelaces, in case anyone was looking at her. She didn't need people thinking she was a freak on the first day of school.

"Hey, kiddo," Christopher said finally. She heard the voice as though it were a thought in her own head—yet the voice was Christopher's.

"Hey, Christopher," she said, instantly relieved. She didn't speak out loud, but "thought" the words instead.

"Got a bad case of nerves, huh?" Christopher said.

"How did you know?" Olivia asked.

"I had a pretty hairy ride coming in, so I knew something was up," Christopher said. "Felt a little like I was sitting in the back of a New York City cab, going seventy and hitting every pothole."

"Oh, sorry about that," Olivia said. It was an unfortunate side effect of being able to talk with each other: If Olivia was feeling bad, it was harder for Christopher to come through.

"No problem, kiddo," Christopher said. "So, what is this place, anyway?" Olivia felt her head being tugged upward, so she knew Christopher was looking up at the building.

"The new school," Olivia replied miserably. "You know . . . the one for *talented* kids. The one I have no right to set foot in."

"Baloney! You've got plenty of talent, Olivia."

"Yeah? Like what?"

"You can belch the entire alphabet, if I remember correctly," Christopher said.

"Oh, you're hysterical today," Olivia said dryly. "Anyway, they'll probably kick me out by the end of the day."

"Then there's nothing to worry about, is there?" Christopher said.

"Nothing except public humiliation." Olivia sighed.

"Nah. Just think about it, kiddo," Christopher said. "For most of the seventh graders, this is the first new school they've been to since kindergarten. They'll be too nervous to pay any attention to you. You, on the other hand, are an old pro at being in new schools. You'll coast right through this."

"Yeah, maybe," Olivia said, not entirely convinced. Still, his words managed to take the edge off her nerves. "So, what have you been up to lately?" she asked, to change the subject. "Are you working with anyone new?"

According to Christopher, dead people didn't just lounge around all day, doing whatever they wanted. Most of them were assigned to different jobs, which always struck Olivia as very unfair. Christopher's job was to help people who had just died adjust to the Spirit World. And since he had a lot of patience, he generally was assigned the most difficult spirits.

"I'm in between assignments this week," Christopher replied. "The last woman they had me work with refused to believe she was dead. She thought she was dreaming, and she kept kicking me in the ankles to see if I was real."

Suddenly Olivia was aware of a pair of large, hooded green eyes inches from her own face.

"Geez!" Olivia cried, drawing back so quickly that she smashed her lower back against the edge of the step behind her.

"Were you sleeping?" The girl in front of her had a low, husky voice, almost like a boy's, and tar-black hair with too-short bangs. She was wearing a pair of overalls that were obviously hand sewn, cut out of red velvet.

"What?" Olivia said, confused.

"The school buzzer's been going off. You were just sitting there, staring off into space."

Olivia heard the buzzer now. It was so loud she was amazed that she could have missed it.

"I thought you might be sleeping," the girl said.

"With my eyes open?" Olivia shot back incredulously.

"*I* sleep with my eyes open."

That must be a frightening sight, Olivia thought. The girl's eyes were eerie enough when they were awake. They were large and round, and her heavy lids slanted down at an angle, like busted window shades.

"I trained myself to do it," the girl added.

"Fascinating," Olivia muttered.

The girl stared at Olivia for a moment. "Do you mean that? Or are you just being rude to me?" she asked.

Well, what kind of a question is that! Olivia thought, squirming under the girl's stare. Of course she was just being rude. But it was positively indecent to put a person on the spot like that! In her head she could hear her brother softly laughing.

"No, it really is fascinating," Olivia demurred. What else could she say, after all?

"What's your name?" the girl wanted to know.

When Olivia told her, the girl stared at her for a few seconds, then asked, "Do you like chicken salad, Olivia?"

"I guess."

"So do I. Do you want to have lunch with me today?"

"Oh . . . I don't know," Olivia hedged.

"When will you know?"

"All right, fine, I'll have lunch with you," Olivia said, just to get rid of her.

The girl smiled. Her eyes didn't crinkle up at all when she smiled, like a normal person. "My name is Stella. I'll meet you in front of the water fountain on the first floor."

"Yup."

"She seems like a nice kid," Christopher said after Stella had left. "And now you know what you'll be doing for lunch."

"Yeah. Avoiding the water fountain on the first floor. Anyway, I'd better go in." She hauled her fat backpack back onto her shoulders. "And by the way, I was never able to belch past the letter *G*."

"Probably a good thing, don't you think?"

"Yeah, probably," Olivia admitted.